# OF SPICE AND MEN

A NORA BLACK MIDLIFE PSYCHIC MYSTERY
BOOK 10

RENEE GEORGE

BARKSIDE OF THE MOON PRESS

# ACKNOWLEDGMENTS

I have to thank sooo many people for this series!

First, I want to thank my critique partners, Robbin Clubb and Robyn Peterman, for tirelessly reviewing every chapter as I wrote the book and giving me so much feedback. This book is amazing because of them!

Second, to the readers and my Rebels, what would be the point without you all? I am so happy and blessed to have you guys in my corner!

Third, but not least, coffee. Thank you, strong black coffee, for once again being there for me through every step of the writing process. You are a wonderful gift to me and humanity.

*For Erin*
*My Canadian Drag-loving Sister*
*From Another Mister*

Of Spice and Men

A Nora Black Midlife Psychic Mystery Book 10

Copyright © 2025 by Renee George

Publisher: Barkside of the Moon Press

Print ISBN: 978-1-947177-54-3

**My name is Nora Black. I'm fifty-six years old, and I'm having the midlife adventure of my life.**

I'm all set for the ultimate winter escape: an adults-only cruise with my sweetheart Ezra, and my best friends Gilly and Pippa, along with their husbands. We are ready to hit the high seas for sun, fun, and definitely no crime-solving. The plan is simple... cocktails, sunsets, and endless laughter.

But you know what they say about the best-laid plans...

When one of our tablemates ends up face down in the hydrotherapy pool, It's looking more and more likely his suspicious death will be declared an accidental drowning.

But my psychic nose says otherwise—this is murder.

Now, with the clock ticking before we reach foreign soil, I'll have to use my aroma mojo to sniff out the truth. It looks like it's up to us to unravel the mystery before the killer gets away with murder.

So much for smooth sailing!

# CHAPTER
# ONE

I slid open the glass door of our balcony suite and stepped out onto the narrow deck, just big enough for a small table and two chairs. Luckily, the suite, decorated in soft, neutral tones of sandy beige and ocean blue, was much roomier. It was large enough for a plush king-sized bed, a cozy sitting area, and a spa-like bathroom with a moderately large shower with marble finishes.

The hum of the ship's engines mingled with the faint rush of waves. We'd left Tampa behind two hours earlier, and now, with no land in sight, the *Lady Voyager* cut through the water, smooth and steady, leaving a trail of white foam.

Ezra stepped out after me, wrapping his arms around my waist from behind and pulling me close. His warmth contrasted with the cool sea air, and he kissed my ear, his lips brushing just enough to make me shiver. "I still can't believe you've never been on a cruise before, Nora."

"What can't you believe about it?" I asked, leaning back into him as the breeze lifted his faintly earthy cologne and mixed it with the ocean air.

"You just always seem so..." He hesitated, and I could feel the grin in his voice.

"Old?" I teased.

Ezra laughed, the deep, rich sound vibrating through his chest against my back. "No." He turned me in his arms to face him, the sun glinting in his emerald-green eyes. "You've just done so much in life already. You're confident. Accomplished... it's hard to picture you missing out on anything."

I chuckled, sliding my hands over his shoulders and lacing my fingers behind his neck. The breeze rustled the open collar of his button-down shirt, revealing a hint of chest hair. "After this, we can get me a shirt that says, *Been there, done that, got the T-shirt.*"

"Anything you want." His lips curved into a lopsided grin, but his gaze drifted past me, out over the endless water. The setting sun layered the sky with shades of orange, pink, and deep purple. "I can't believe we're on vacation. Like, an actual *leave everything behind and sail into paradise* kind of vacation. It feels surreal."

"I'm just glad we could all make the time to do it," I said, following his gaze. The ocean stretched forever as if nothing else existed but us and the water.

The eight-day cruise from Tampa to Cozumel, Belize City, Roatán, the Grand Caymans then back to Tampa was a dream none of us had realized we needed until it came to life. It started as a casual conversation at

Christmas after our town of Garden Cove had experienced a week-long ice storm that had us all cussing the freezing weather. Pippa had mentioned the tropics, half-joking, and Ezra had chimed in, saying he'd always wanted to go on a cruise. The idea snowballed from there, each of us adding our own enthusiasm for the topic to the mix—Gilly and Scott's scuba-diving ambitions, Jordy's love for snorkeling, and my desperate longing to escape January's icy grip. By the time we toasted the New Year, we'd already booked an eight-day adults-only cruise to the sunny Caribbean.

Here we were in late March, and the cold and snow were just frozen memories that had already started to thaw. I closed my eyes, listening to the faint cries of seagulls in the distance and giving in to the gentle swaying of the ship beneath my feet.

"Thank you," I said.

"For what?" Ezra asked.

"For nothing and everything."

He smoothed my unruly hair away from my face, then dipped his head, his broad, firm lips brushing against mine. I melted against his body, enjoying the way his hands slid down my back as he deepened the kiss.

"Oh, God," Gilly said. "I'm going to be sick. Again."

I looked at Ezra and shook my head before turning to find Gilly on her balcony, which was connected to ours. She looked pale and, frankly, a little green around the gills.

Her husband, Scott, trailed behind, extending his

open hand toward her. "I told you to take these before we got on the boat." In the middle of his palm were two small white pills.

"But they make me sleepy," she whined. "Besides, there was no way to know for certain I'd get seasick."

"Oh, I don't know, love," he told her. "There were some clues." His expression was a study of practiced patience. "Like the fact that you get carsick and carnival ride sick, and the last time we went out on my fishing boat, you chummed the water."

When I tried not to laugh, it came out as a snort.

"Don't you start, Nora," Gilly said, betrayal in her voice, as she took the seasickness pills from Scott. "You're supposed to be on my side."

"I'm one hundred percent on your side," I told her. "You've never been on a cruise. There was no way of knowing if the constant swaying of a giant ship would trigger your sensitivity to motion."

She looked at me as if she were trying to figure out whether I was being sarcastic, then said, "Exactly. I couldn't have known."

Ezra's chuckle was soft and pleasant. I gave him a gentle elbow to the gut.

Scott stared at his wife with a mix of adoration and worry. "It shouldn't take too long to kick in. You'll be feeling better in no time."

"I'll be ready for a nap," she complained. "I want to be fabulous for dinner tonight."

"You're always fabulous," Pippa said, stepping out

onto the balcony on the other side of Gilly's. "Even sleepy."

Gilly smiled, briefly mollified, then her eyes bulged as she put her hand over her mouth and ran back into her room. Scott and Ezra exchanged looks before Scott hurried inside after her.

"I hope she's not sick the whole cruise," Pippa said. "That would be a complete bummer."

"I hate you," a woman shouted from the room on the other side of mine.

"Stupid cow," I heard a man with a British accent shout. "I told you no the first time, but you're too dumb to understand the word. Let me spell it out for you. N. O. No. It means it's not happening. It's never happening, and no matter how many times you ask, the answer isn't changing, so quit crying over something we've already discussed."

I glanced at Pippa, then Ezra, then back to Pippa. I could feel my eyes bulging from my head. This was coming from the room next to ours, and while their balcony door was closed, their voices were coming through loud and clear.

"Holy crap," I mouthed.

Pippa winced. "I know, right?" she mouthed back.

The sliding glass door slid open on their balcony, and we all looked over as a teary-eyed woman staggered out to the rail. The bombshell beauty with caramel brown hair held her fist to her chest as she looked out over the water before looking around and noticing she wasn't alone.

With a sniffle, she said, "Oh, hi, sorry." She gently wiped at her face with her fingertips, then patted the area under her eyes dry. "The majesty of the sea. It always gets me."

The majesty of the sea and a nasty man, I thought. "No worries," I told her. "I completely understand. The gorgeous view is enough to make anyone emotional."

"I know I'm feeling emotional," Pippa added in solidarity.

"Who's emotional?" Gilly said, stumbling back onto her balcony. Then she noticed the stranger. "Hi there." Her eyes bulged and her hand flew back over her mouth. "'Scuse me," she gutted out before running back inside.

I gave the woman an apologetic wince. "She's got motion sickness."

"Poor dear," she said, tucking her chin. Her small bow mouth pursed for a second. "Do you all know each other?"

"Yes," Pippa answered. "We're best friends and business partners. This is our first vacation in years."

"Well, a *real* vacation," Jordy said. "Nothing but sun and fun, with no problems to solve other than where to set our stuff down at the pool."

The woman sniffled again. "How nice for you all."

"I'm Nora Black." I gestured to Ezra. "And this is Ezra. Over there," I pointed to my friends, "are Pippa and her husband, Jordy. Our seasick friend is Gilly, and she's here with her husband, Scott."

"I'm Callie," the woman said. "My husband, Sebastian, and I are here for our fifth wedding anniversary."

*Yikes.* Only five years married, and he was already calling her names like *stupid cow?* I felt sorry for Callie.

"Happy anniversary," Ezra said.

She blushed and averted her gaze. "I better get back inside."

After she went in, I whispered, "That was super sad."

Ezra nodded.

Pippa waved me over. When I was close, she hissed, "That's *Calliope Grant.*"

I gave her a quizzical look.

She shook her head, looking exasperated. "She's a vocalist who won *Ultimate Singer of America* six years ago. You know, the national contest where the winner gets a recording contract with Zeta Records and a global tour."

I shrugged. "I've never heard of her."

However, I *had* heard of the show. It was one of the ones Ari, Gilly's daughter, loved to watch. "Do I know any of her songs?"

"Doubtful." Pippa shook her head. "Her husband, Billy Grant, fell from a hotel balcony the night of the finale..." Conspiratorially, she added, "...while she was on stage, getting her accolades."

"Her *husband*?" Ezra asked. "Why wasn't he at the show with her? I mean, the finale seems like a big deal to miss."

"Good question," Pippa answered. "With no good explanation, considering he had been given a ticket. His death was listed as undetermined." She finger-quoted the last word. "But the investigation never uncovered any proof of foul play."

I arched a brow. "And how do you know all this?"

*"The Reality of Getting Away With Murder with Mimi and Serge,"* she said as if it should mean something to me.

"It's a podcast," Jordy clarified. "It explores suspicious deaths and murders related to reality stars." The corner of his mouth quirked into a half-smile. "Pippa and I listen to it in the evening after we put the kids to bed."

"Talk about setting a mood." I smirked. "And we're bunking next to one of the subjects of the podcast. How wild is that?" I would've laughed if it hadn't been so surreal. "You said Callie's husband's death was undetermined? Her alibi seems pretty airtight. You can't murder someone if you're on stage in front of millions of people. Why did his death make the murder show?"

Pippa's gaze narrowed, and her voice lowered even more. "Because within a year of his death, she married the head judge, Sebastian Caldwell, a record producer from England. After that season, Sebastian, who had been their most popular judge and one of the show's producers, was out. They replaced him with country singer Clint Wade. Sebastian is still listed as a creator and co-producer, but the show has distanced itself from him." Her cadence sped up, and her voice went up an octave in pitch. "On top of all that, Mimi and Serge, the podcasters, were anonymously sent a secret recording of Callie's husband confronting her about sleeping her way to the final, and Callie told him she wished he was dead. It was brutal."

"Wowza." I blinked a few times. "So, do you think the guy next door calling her names is the judge, Sebastian Caldwell?"

Pippa shrugged and nodded. "She and Sebastian did get married, and that guy yelling has a British accent."

I glanced at Callie's empty balcony. "That's nuts."

"I wonder if she had her husband murdered or maybe her new husband arranged it. An older man enamored by the ingenue and willing to go to any lengths to be with her." Pippa cocked her brow at me. "Maybe you could—"

I gave a sharp shake of my head. "That sounds more like a gothic romance than a mystery. Besides, I'm on vacation," I told her. "I am not going to investigate anything other than where I can find the best margarita on this ship."

Pippa frowned. "Spoilsport."

Ezra chuckled as he put his arms around me again. "Nora's nose is officially off duty."

"Fine," my blonde bestie said with a pout. "But that doesn't mean I won't keep an ear out for intrigue."

"You do you," I told her with a laugh. I couldn't help but wonder why a famous record producer-slash-tv personality wasn't in one of the penthouse suites or a villa on the ship. I mean, our concierge sunset suites were nice, but they weren't rich people nice. I was about to say as much to Pippa when Scott walked out onto the balcony.

"I'm not sure Gilly's going to make dinner tonight," he announced. "The nausea isn't letting up."

"Aww, bummer. I hope she feels better soon," I said sympathetically. "Is there anything we can do to help her?"

"Not unless you can keep the ship from rocking," he replied.

I waved a hand at him. "That's beyond my scope of expertise."

"Hopefully, she'll feel better later tonight or at least by morning," Scott said.

"Hopefully," I agreed. "Or this vacation will be one miserable day after another for her." *Poor Gilly.* She'd been so excited about the cruise. I hated that it was off to such a bad start for her. "Will you be going to dinner or staying in with Gilly?"

Scott shook his head. "If she can't go, I'll skip it too. I don't want to leave her alone. We'll have something sent to the room."

I smiled. "Good man."

He smirked, giving me a wry look. "I try."

And he *succeeded*. After kissing a lot of toads, including a bastard of an ex-husband, Gilly had finally found her Prince Charming. I'm ashamed to admit that I held my breath a little, waiting for the other shoe to drop with Scott. But he had repeatedly proven to be as good as he was true. The best part? He loved Gilly the way she deserved to be loved.

"There are still a few hours," I told him. "Maybe she'll perk up by then."

"Maybe." He grimaced when we all heard her puke again. "I'd better get back inside."

"Do you want me to go to the sundries shop and get something else for her stomach?" I asked.

"I've given her a dose of meclizine," he said. "I don't want to overdo the medicine."

"What about some lemon-lime soda?" Ezra asked. "It can help with upset stomachs."

"Or ginger ale," Pippa added. "That's what my pediatrician recommended when JayJay got that stomach virus." JayJay was Pippa's four-year-old daughter.

"Both of those are good options," Scott said. "If you can find either, it could help."

"And some saltines," I added. "Those always help me when I feel icky in the tummy."

"Yep," Scott said. "Those too, if they have them."

I took Ezra's hand. "We'll go see what we can find."

Pippa nodded. "You guys go to the shop for crackers, and Jordy and I will head to the bar for the lemon-lime soda." She gestured to their wrists. They'd bought the unlimited non-alcoholic drink package because Jordy was over fifteen years sober. "If they have ginger ale, we'll get that too."

"Ginger ale is used in a lot of mixed drinks, so it's probably a good gamble." I turned my gaze to Scott. "We've got our mission, Doc. We'll be back soon."

He grinned. "Gilly's lucky she's got such great friends."

"We're *all* lucky," I said. "She'd do it for us."

"I would," Gilly yelled from inside the cabin. Then she uttered, "Oh, Gawd," and began to retch again.

I tugged on Ezra. "Time to go."

# CHAPTER

# TWO

The sundries shop was packed with vacationers purchasing essentials—forgotten toothbrushes, travel-sized shampoos, and overpriced sunscreen. Ezra and I shouldered our way to the snack shelf, scanning for something Gilly could stomach.

"They've got peanut butter crackers, cheese ones, and crackers coated in every spice under the sun, but no saltines," I complained, exasperated.

"What about some peppermints?" Ezra asked, plucking a bag from the display. "They're good for nausea, right?"

"Definitely," I said, more impressed than necessary.

He grinned. "Hey, I know stuff."

I leaned in and nudged him with my shoulder. "Yes, you do."

His green eyes danced with humor. "Which variety, though?"

"Better safe than sorry." I grabbed spearmint, peppermint, and Wintermint, then made my way to the checkout.

As we stepped out of the shop, something caught my eye. Through the glass storefront of *Pompier*, the duty-free perfume and beauty store, I spotted my balcony neighbor, Callie. She stood inches from a tall, dark-haired man, smiling as she held a bottle of perfume in her hand. He reached up and tucked a loose lock of hair behind her ear, his touch lingering.

"What are you smiling about?" Ezra asked as we passed by.

I gave a subtle nod toward the window. "Looks like our neighbors have made up."

Ezra glanced inside, then chuckled. "That's all it takes? A fancy bottle of perfume, and all's forgiven?"

"Not hardly." I snorted. "If you ever talk to me the way he spoke to her, you'll be hitchhiking from a buoy back to the mainland."

"Noted," he said with a grin.

We stepped onto the elevator, joining a young couple who stood close, fingers intertwined. The woman had the warm, tropical scent of coconut and pineapple clinging to her skin—sunscreen or body spray, I wasn't sure. The fragrance hit me like a slap as a vision sharpened around me, pulling me into a sun-drenched world.

*A man and a woman lounge on a beach, golden light spilling over them. Their faces remain blurred, like always. The woman is lying on her back on a vibrant, oversized beach towel, her skin glistening with a sheen of sunscreen and her pale blonde hair spilling onto the sand. The man with shoulder-length, light brown hair kneels beside her, his strong hands smoothing lotion over her legs slow and deliberate.*

*"God, you smell good enough to eat," he murmurs, his voice thick with warmth.*

*She giggles, a soft, lilting sound that carries on the ocean breeze. "I knew you'd like it."*

*He leans closer, inhaling deeply. "Piña coladas."*

*"And getting caught in the rain," she teases, turning her head just enough for me to catch the tilt of her smile.*

*But then, something shifts. The man hesitates, his hands pausing on her thighs. The playful energy dims, replaced by something heavier. "Do you think we can really do this?" he asks, his voice quieter now, uncertain.*

*She doesn't hesitate. "We can." She reaches for his hand, threading her fingers through his. "We have to."*

*Lifting her other hand, she flashes a stunning pear-cut diamond ring. The sun catches on its facets, sending a shimmer of light across her tanned skin. "Only six more months."*

*His grip tightens as he lifts her hand to his lips, pressing a kiss to her palm. "Only six more months." There's something dark on his shoulder, and as he leans over his partner. I can see it's a shield. It's familiar. A shield with a yellow top half and red and white stripes going vertical on the bottom. Still, I can't quite place where I've seen it before.*

*The woman turns over onto her stomach. "Do my back, please." On her right shoulder is the twin of his tattoo.*

*The vision lingers a heartbeat longer before I'm yanked back to the present.*

I sucked in a breath, lightheaded. Ezra's arm brushed mine as he steadied me. His brow arched in a silent question.

I shook my head slightly, not wanting to explain in front of the strangers. I had thought the vision belonged to the couple, but their hair was different. Hair changes. No big deal. I glanced at the woman's left hand. She had a pear-shaped diamond engagement ring in front of her wedding band, but I couldn't be certain it was the same one from the memory. I looked at the man's wrist for the tattoo, but it wasn't there either. The memory must've been for someone who had passed them in the hall and smelled the coconut-pineapple combo. It wouldn't be the first time a strong emotion clung to a scent after the originator was no longer around.

The elevator doors slid open, and the couple exited ahead of us. Ezra and I followed, only to realize we were all heading in the same direction down the long corridor. The pair stopped a few doors from ours at an interior room across the hall.

"See ya," the woman said with a slight wave at us as they went inside.

I gave a slight wave back as Ezra opened the door to our room.

"So, what did you see," he asked as we went inside.

I shrugged. "The usual," I told him. "Just a slice of life. A couple on the beach somewhere warm and having a moment. Before marriage, if I had to guess, but maybe shortly after they were engaged."

He narrowed his gaze at me. "Those slice-of-life visions don't usually take it out of you."

"This one packed a punch for sure." I sighed. "The moment must have been really important to whoever they were."

"You don't think it was the couple in the elevator?"

I shrugged then shook my head. "Right builds, but everything else was wrong."

"Hmm."

"It happens." But I couldn't shake the intensity of the memory.

"Well, I'm happy it wasn't something more nefarious." Ezra put his arm around my shoulder and chuckled softly. "Usually, when you have an intense reaction to a vision, there's a killer on the loose."

I leaned against him. "Not this time," I told him. "Just two people with big feelings for each other."

He smiled, his green eyes softening as he met my gaze. "I understand that feeling."

Out on the balcony, we beckoned Scott. "No crackers, but we got these." I handed him the mints with an apologetic smile. "These are supposed to help with nausea, right?"

"Thanks," he said, taking the bags and giving us a grateful smile. "It definitely won't hurt. Pippa and Jordy beat you back," Scott added. "They found both lemon-lime and ginger ale. Between the drinks, the mints, and the meclizine, hopefully, we'll get our girl back in form."

RENEE GEORGE

Gilly appeared in the doorway as if beckoned, wrapped in a light blanket, sipping a can of ginger ale through a straw. Some color had returned to her cheeks.

"You look a lot less green," I observed. "That's a good sign."

"We'll see," she murmured, rubbing her temple before yawning. "I think the motion sickness pill has triggered my nap-reflex." She crooked her head back, and the bones in her neck cracked. "The bed is calling me hard."

"You should go lie down," Scott suggested. "When you wake up, you'll feel much better."

"I hope you're right." She gave her husband a quick peck on the cheek, then turned to us, shooing with one hand. "You guys go, get ready, shower, have fun...whatever. I don't want to be the party pooper."

I smiled. "There's no party you could ever poop."

Pippa poked her head out of her sliding glass door, her eyes wide and eager. "We could properly explore the upper decks before dinner."

"Good plan," I agreed.

"I'm up for it," Ezra said.

"Great!" Pippa clapped her hands. "Jordy and I will meet you guys out in the hall."

---

"I can't believe I'm on a cruise," Jordy said as we walked along the rail of the Lido deck. "I honestly never had it on my bucket list, but until a few years ago, my only bucket list item was to never get high again." I knew he was only semi-joking. The man worked hard on his sobriety. He even held NA meetings after hours in his coffee shop.

"I've always wanted to try one," Ezra told him. "A cruise, not getting high." He chuckled. "But I've never had a reason to do it." He glanced at me. "Glad I have one now."

Jordy grinned as his eyes lit up. "This is like a second honeymoon for us.

Pippa flashed him with a dazzling smile. "Every day with you is a honeymoon."

He laughed. "Oh, yeah. I'm a real picnic." His long hair was up in a double-braided man bun. It made him look like a Viking preparing for battle. He had the height and the muscle to go with the hair. Although I'd noticed since baby number two, Jordy had started to get a little bit of a dad bod. Pippa had told me the extra girth made her husband even more handsome.

Pippa elbowed him. "I'm happy."

He gave her a crooked smile. "That's all I ever want."

Ezra's hand slipped into mine. "I'm happy, too."

The wind whipped my hair into my face before I could respond, and a noise of surprise squeaked out of my throat at the powerful gust. Ezra tugged me against him and held me until my feet were steady beneath me. "Wow, that was something else."

"Do you think a storm is blowing in?" Pippa asked.

"There's a few dark clouds out," Ezra said, pointing at the horizon. "Hopefully, it won't amount to anything."

"They weren't calling for storms when we left port,"

Jordy added. "We are moving fast through the ocean. I'm sure the wind kicks up everything now and then."

"You're probably right." We continued on our way, weaving in and out of other passenger's paths as we passed the pool area. I recognized a familiar face lounging on a deck chair. "Hey, that's our neighbor, Callie." I looked around and didn't see her husband. "I guess Sebastian stayed in the room."

"What are you talking about," Pippa whispered. "That's him right there in the deck chair next to her."

I glanced over, trying not to gawk at the older man in the straw hat, wearing zinc sunscreen on his nose. His skin was a jaundiced orange, his legs skinny, and his stomach had the tale-tell pooch of someone who'd pickled his liver.

I shook my head. "That's not her husband."

"It's Sebastian Caldwell," Pippa argued. "I watched Callie's entire season after we listened to the podcast. I'd recognize his bad spray tan anywhere."

I gave Ezra a pointed look. "Am I crazy?"

"Nope." He arched a brow. "Definitely not the guy she was hanging out with in the perfume shop."

"She was with another man?" Pippa's eyes went wide. "Why am I just hearing about this now?"

"Because until now, I thought it was her husband," I replied. "I didn't know there was anything to tell."

"Holy crap," she rasped. "She's cheating on her husband."

Jordy added, "The way he was talking to her, you can hardly blame her."

Pippa rubbed her hands eagerly. "Do you think she met the man today, or did her lover book a trip to be with her?"

"Or maybe I mistook a perfectly innocent moment for something else," I told them. "All the man did was move her hair behind her ear." She had looked so happy as they gazed at each other. "Maybe she's just a flirt."

"Maybe," Ezra agreed. He held his hands out, palms up. "Maybe not."

"If you see this guy again, point him out," Pippa demanded.

I snorted. "You betcha." However, there were hundreds of people on the ship. What were the odds we'd run into the guy again?

---

A FEW HOURS LATER, we were seated at the dinner table in the main dining room. The décor felt expensive with its crisp white linens, beautiful creamy magnolia center-pieces surrounded by glass-incased pillar candles, along with gold chairs and crystal chandeliers. There was an elaborate fountain at the center of the room of a sea maiden holding a vessel above her head as water poured over her and into a pool at her feet.

Ezra pulled out my chair before taking his own seat beside me. The soft hum of conversation and clinking glasses filled the air. A runner in a white uniform offered water to the table, and once glasses were filled, we began our introductions.

21

The woman with soft blonde hair curled neatly to frame her face smiled warmly. "Carl and Augusta Franks," she said, her voice gentle and friendly as she touched the locket on the gold necklace she wore. "We're celebrating our fortieth anniversary."

"Congratulations," I said. "Forty years is amazing."

Next to them, the young couple leaned in eagerly. The woman, barely in her twenties, had a sweet, sunburned face and bright eyes. "I'm Helena, and this is Jasper," she said, her voice bubbling with excitement. "We're on our honeymoon. It's our first time out of the country."

Jasper nodded, his arm slung affectionately around her chair. "We met in college. Never thought we'd end up in a place like this." His grin was easy and contagious.

"Congratulations," Pippa said sincerely from across the table. "The first big trip together is always special."

Callie and Sebastian, went next. She barely looked like the same woman we'd seen earlier. Her sleek chestnut hair was styled into a glossy bob, her makeup was Hollywood-perfect, and there was a confident, poised air about her that hadn't been there when she'd been on the balcony. Her emerald-green dress matched her eyes perfectly.

"Callie Caldwell," she said with a nod, gesturing to the man beside her. "My husband, Sebastian."

Sebastian, who looked like he belonged on a yacht catalog cover, gave a brief but polite nod. "Nice to meet everyone." His strongly accented voice was smooth, but his tone felt detached, like he'd rather be anywhere else.

"We met earlier," I told her. "We're your neighbors."

Her eyes lit up with recognition before her cheeks colored in a way that even makeup couldn't cover. "Oh, yes, that's right," she stammered.

I smiled at the older couple to my left. "Hi, I'm Nora, and this is my partner Ezra. First time cruisers, and our first big trip together as well," I said, giving a nod to the honeymooners.

"I'm Pippa, and this is my husband Jordy." Pippa gave a friendly wave. "Same as Nora. First big trip. First cruise."

"Good evening," a man in tight black pants, and a white shirt that hugged his chest greeted, drawing our attention. "I'm Ramone Reyes, the ship's dance instructor, and we'll have our first class in the ballroom tonight after dinner." He set a short stack of cards on the table. "I hope you will all join me."

I had to fight to keep the look of O.M.G. out of my eyes as I turned to face Pippa. She was beaming a smile at the tall, dark-haired, handsome Ramone, so I had to hold my stare until she finally glanced my way.

Her brows dipped as our eyes met.

Mine raised a little as I shifted my eyes toward Callie then back to Pippa.

Her eyes widened when she picked up what I was putting down, and I gave a barely perceptible nod of confirmation.

This was the guy. The one who'd been intimately close with Callie in the perfume shop. Callie acted as if it were the first time she'd met Ramone. Her performance was natural and convincing. If I hadn't seen her earlier in the day with him, I would've bet good money they'd never laid eyes on each other before this moment. It told me one very important thing about the woman.

She was a liar and a good one at that.

# THREE

After Ramone moved on to the next table, I picked up the menu and scanned the courses. There was a list of starters, main courses, and desserts. At the top of the menu was the chef's recommendation of scallops topped with butter, crab, and bacon crumbles starter, blackened grouper over wild whole grain rice as the main course served with roasted asparagus and topped with mango salsa, and, for dessert, chocolate lava cake with tequila lime coconut macaroons. All the options sounded like winners to me.

I couldn't help but muse about how Callie and Ramone interacted. Their body language had carried the casualness of two strangers...so casual that I began to doubt what I'd seen earlier. Maybe it hadn't been the dance instructor in the shop with her. Perhaps it had been someone else entirely. My eyesight was twenty-twenty thanks to corrective surgery, but the shopping area had been crowded, and I'd only glimpsed Callie and the man through a glass partition. Could I have been mistaken?

Ezra's hand slid onto my knee, giving it a gentle squeeze. When I looked over, he nodded toward Augusta, seated with her husband to our left. That's when I realized she'd asked me a question.

"I'm sorry," I said, my face warming with a flush of embarrassment. "I totally spaced out. It must be jet lag. My brain's all over the place."

"Don't worry about it, dear," Augusta replied warmly. "I was only making small talk."

"She asked what you do," Ezra prompted softly.

"Oh." I straightened up, offering a polite smile. "I own a little shop in Garden Cove. I make soaps, lotions, and other homemade beauty products." I gestured to my right. "Pippa's my right hand. Honestly, she's my right, my left, and both feet. I couldn't run the shop without her."

"Nora was the top regional sales manager for one of the biggest beauty companies in the country before taking on this venture," Pippa chimed in with a playful cluck of her tongue. "Believe me when I say she doesn't need me."

I rolled my eyes. "Pippa was my executive assistant back then. Trust me, without her, I wouldn't have been able to do what I did. She's a great partner."

"Well, it sounds like a mutual admiration society," Carl said with a chuckle. His thick, gray eyebrows were neatly trimmed, and his manicured nails were smooth and clean. Hands that looked like they'd never seen a day of hard labor.

Just then, the servers appeared, weaving between tables. An elegant, slender black woman approached us, her face lit up with a radiant smile.

"Welcome to the *Lady Voyage* fine dining experience. My name is Charise," she said, her voice smooth and melodic. "I'll be your steward all week in the main dining room. It's my pleasure to serve you. Can I get your drink and food orders?"

"I'll take the chef's recommendation," I said when she pointed at me. "And a glass of your Riesling."

"Sounds good to me, too." Ezra nodded. "But I'll take the Pinot Grigio."

I made a face. Pinot probably paired better with seafood than the German Riesling, but it was too dry a wine for my taste. I had the palette of a seventeen-year-old knocking back Boone Farm's Tickle Pink. In other words, I liked my wine sweet.

Pippa ordered the Ceasar salad, herb-crusted pork medallion, and cheesecake. Jordy ordered similarly but swapped the pork for a petite filet. They both asked for iced tea to drink.

Charise nodded to Callie and Sebastian next. She practically sang her question, "And what can I get for you?" She had a lovely voice, but Sebastian didn't even look up when he ordered.

"I'll take the scallops, the medium rare steak, and the tiramisu." He held up his menu for Charise to take. "And a glass of your Cabernet Sauvignon."

"Very good, sir," Charise replied, taking the menu. Her cheerful expression had turned into a scowl. As if realizing her face was speaking volumes, she quickly replaced the sour expression with a wide smile that didn't reach her eyes.

Callie gave the steward an apologetic nod. "I'll take the house salad, the grouper, and the lava cake."

"And to drink?"

"The Moscato." Callie flashed me a smile. "I like my wine like I like my men, cheap and sweet."

She giggled. Sebastian rolled his eyes.

After our steward left, Pippa's eyes narrowed. "Why does she look familiar?"

"Maybe she has one of those faces," Augusta mused.

Pippa tapped her cheek as she worked to access the memory connection. "Maybe, but I should know who she is."

I look to my left at Augusta and Carl. "I told you what I do. It's your turn."

"I was a pediatrician," Carl responded.

"He's being modest. Carl was one of the best pediatric surgeons in the country," Augusta added with a hint of pride. "We both retired five years ago, and doctors worldwide still reach out to him for consultations."

Carl, his wire-rimmed glasses slipping down his nose, chuckled. "She means I'm retired. Auggie still runs the household like a drill sergeant." His eyes twinkled, earning a playful swat from his wife.

Ezra laughed. "Sounds like a good balance."

"I think performing surgery on children might get

you a sainthood." Pippa grinned. "What was your specialty?"

Carl's smile matched hers. "Gastroenterology."

"A stomach doctor," I translated. "That must've been so interesting." I wondered if Scott had heard of him. "We have a doctor in our group." I gestured at the two empty seats at the table. "He's back in the cabin with his wife. They were supposed to be at dinner tonight, but she's got a bad case of motion sickness."

"It'll pass when she gets her sea legs," Augusta said sympathetically. "I used to feel queasy when we first started cruising."

Pippa nodded her head, her expression sympathetic. "Gilly didn't want to risk getting sick at dinner. Can't say as I blame her."

I nodded, remembering the pale, miserable look on Gilly's face earlier. "Probably for the best. Hopefully, she'll be up for tomorrow."

"And what about you?" I asked her, curious. "You said you were retired too?"

"Augusta was a trophy wife," Carl teased, placing his hand gently over hers. The older woman's ring finger glittered with "Still is."

"Aww," Pippa cooed. "That's so sweet."

"Carl," she said with a headshake and a smile. "I'm a retired attorney."

"Criminal or civil?" Ezra asked.

Augusta gave him a friendly but assessing look. "I started as a criminal attorney but ended my career in private practice as a civil litigator. What about you?" she asked him.

"I'm a detective."

"Private?" Helena asked.

He shook his head. "I'm the head of special investigations for the Garden Cove P.D. It doesn't get much more public than that."

"You must have some interesting stories to tell," Jasper said, joining the conversation.

Ezra shrugged. "A few, but I promised Nora this trip was going to be all fun and sun and no business."

"How long does it take to cook a bloody steak?" Sebastian muttered under his breath. He and Callie were wedged between the honeymooners and the older couple, and he shifted uncomfortably when he noticed the attention turning toward him.

"Don't mind my Sebbie," Callie said, giving him an affectionate pat on the arm. "He gets cranky when he's hungry."

Sebastian shot her a sour look but cleared his throat and sat up straighter as if his posture alone might summon the food faster. He glanced around the dining room, his expression tight with impatience. "The least they could do is bring our drinks"

I shifted my attention to the newlyweds sitting nearby. "Where are you two from?"

"Kentucky," Helena replied cheerfully. "Louisville area."

Her husband nodded. "Go, Cardinals," he added.

"I'm a KU fan, myself," Ezra said, leaning in.

Jordy groaned. "It's MU or nothing, Easy," he said, using Ezra's nickname. "You live in Missouri. Your son literally goes to MU. Dude." He shook his head. "You gotta root for the Tigers."

"Mason doesn't even like sports. Besides..." Ezra pressed a hand to his chest, feigning injury. "...the heart wants what it wants," he said dramatically. "And this heart wants a Rock Chalk, Jayhawk victory."

Jordy barked a laugh. "Not this season. They were out in the first round." He turned to Jasper. "Louisville, too."

"Isn't March Madness over?" Pippa asked.

"Not for another week," Jordy answered.

The guys had started a local pool, including Ezra, Jordy, Scott, and four other basketball-loving friends, for the NCAA tournament the last couple of years. It was twenty dollars to join, and the winner took all. Ezra was convinced he had a shot with Alabama, one of his eight random picks. I didn't follow basketball or any sport, really, but I was great at parroting back whatever Ezra told me.

"Well, too bad you won't be able to keep up with it," I teased.

"There are three sports bars on the ship," Jasper chimed in. "Pretty sure the games will be on in at least one of them."

"Thanks, Jasper," Pippa said with exaggerated sweetness.

He grinned, shaking his head. "Not that I'm encouraging anyone to spend the whole cruise watching TV."

Helena leaned over, her shoulder against Jasper's arm and smirked. "Nice save, babe."

Sebastian scoffed. "You Americans and your obsession with sports."

"Right," Carl jumped in dryly. "Because the Brits aren't at all passionate about soccer."

"Football," Sebastian corrected instinctively. He hesitated, then offered a sheepish smile. "Actually, the only time in my life I ever punched someone was over a Manchester United game." He shook his head. "Bloody Liverpool fans."

For the first time all evening, Sebastian seemed almost human instead of the insufferable, pompous pain in the butt he'd been since dinner started.

"What is it you do, Sebastian?" I asked, even though I already knew the answer.

"I'm on hiatus," he said curtly, clearly not interested in elaborating.

Callie added softly, "He was a record producer for some of the biggest pop stars." There was a flicker of pride in her voice, but something else, too...a hint of regret.

"That's where I've seen you," Augusta said. "Weren't you a judge on that one singing show?"

Pippa, who couldn't help herself, blurted, "Ultimate Singer of America."

Callie's eyes lit up at Pippa's recognition. "His first show was Britain's Got Stars. He put singing competitions on the map."

"You're on hiatus?" I asked.

"I've moved on," Sebastian said briskly. "Bigger and better things."

I knew from Pippa that he'd left the show after Callie's season, and the rumor was that he'd been forced out. Even so, something inside me wouldn't let sleeping dogs lie. "Like what kind of bigger and better things?"

"I'm meeting with investors about a reality show on a cruise ship," he admitted, his eyes sparking with enthusiasm. "A talent competition for the next big cruise act. Winner gets a cash prize and a year-long headliner contract with *Lady Voyage*." He leaned back, looking smug. "It's going to be huge."

Pippa perked up. "I would totally watch that."

"Do you sing or dance?" Callie asked her, amused.

Pippa laughed. "Me? Heck, no. I can't carry a tune to save my life."

"That's not true," Jordy said, nudging her. "You sing with JayJay all the time."

Pippa blushed. "Nobody wants to hear my rendition of *Pink Pony Club,* trust me."

We all laughed, the tension easing as the drinks arrived. The same young man who poured our water delivered the drinks to our table. The conversation shifted to lighter topics. Laughter bubbled up here and there. The wine loosened nerves and tongues while warming the atmosphere.

When Charise arrived back at our table with two assistants carrying two large trays, Pippa leaned in and whispered. "Oh my gosh. I know where I know our steward."

I tucked my chin. "Really?"

"She was on Ultimate Singer of America the year before Callie."

I pivoted my gaze to my friend. "I thought you only watched Callie's season."

"It's possible that I watched more seasons than that."

"Possible?" I chuckled. "Are you sure? Augusta is probably right that she just has one of those faces."

"I know it's her," Pippa whispered. "This is so crazy."

"It's quite the coincidence," I agreed.

"She hates Sebastian."

"Why?"

"He told her that her vocal coach should be blind-folded and put in front of a firing squad for giving her false hope that she could sing." She grimaced. "Well, something to that effect."

"Ouch."

"Yep." Pippa stopped talking when Charise made her way to our side of the table with the food.

Charise set our plates down with a professional smile, but her eyes lingered on Sebastian for a moment longer than necessary. If looks could kill, his medium-rare steak might've come out well-done and laced with vengeance.

Sebastian didn't notice. He was too busy cutting into scallops with enthusiasm. Callie chatted softly with Helena while the rest of us dug into our meals.

"Here, baby," Callie said as she began sorting her salad then plucking green olives from the plate with her fingers and putting them on his scallop plate. "I hate them," she explained to the table, "but Seb loves them."

"I really do." Unceremoniously, Sebastian practically inhaled all five olives she'd transferred over to him, one after another.

I couldn't help but sneak glances at Charise as she moved through the dining room, gracefully balancing trays and topping off wine glasses. If she really was the woman Pippa remembered from *Ultimate Singer of America*, then this was getting more interesting by the second. A former reality show contestant stuck serving the judge who'd humiliated her? You couldn't script that kind of drama.

Ezra leaned toward me, his voice low. "You're staring again."

I blinked and quickly looked down at my plate. "I'm not staring. I'm observing."

His lips twitched. "That's what cops say when they're staring."

"Old habits," I murmured, poking at my scallops.

He squeezed my knee again, a silent reminder to stay present.

The conversation around the table picked up again, led mainly by Carl and Augusta, who had a natural way of making everyone feel included. Augusta was telling a story about a trip they'd taken to Greece when Jasper leaned in toward Sebastian.

"So, this reality show you're pitching, do you think the network will bite?"

Sebastian barely looked up from his plate. "It's not a

question of *if*. They will." He sounded confidently smug. "The cruise industry is untapped reality TV gold. People are stuck together on a floating hotel. A season two pick-up is practically guaranteed."

"Like a more glamorous *Survivor*," Pippa said, clearly intrigued.

"More like *So You Think You Got Talent* meets *Love On The Waves*," Callie added with a smile.

Sebastian made a noise that might've been agreement...or indigestion.

The man was hard to read.

"Do you have talent lined up already?" Jordy asked.

"Got a few leads. Still scouting." Sebastian lifted a shoulder in a noncommittal shrug. "Unfortunately, there are too many people who can't sing their way out of a queue but think they are the next superstar." He grunted a laugh. "Pitiful."

I glanced toward Charise again. She was at the table next to ours, her posture poised but her expression unreadable.

I wondered if Sebastian had recognized her. His words seemed a little too on point with what Pippa had told me.

As I was about to ask Callie more about their reality show plans, Sebastian's loud, startled yelp rang out. Our heads swiveled in his direction as the man jumped up from his chair, frantically brushing at his lap. A dark stain bloomed across his white dress shirt.

"Oh, I'm so sorry!" Charise apologized, her expression appropriately horrified. She held an empty wine glass in one hand, the red liquid clearly no longer inside it. "It slipped."

Sebastian glared at her, his face red. Callie was dabbing uselessly at his shirt and pants with a napkin. "Guess not everyone's cut out for singing or fine dining."

Something flickered in Charise's eyes, something dark and fast, before she turned on her heel and disappeared through the swinging doors to the kitchen.

Pippa leaned in close to me. "I bet ten bucks that wasn't an accident."

I didn't take the bet.

I was pretty sure she was right.

# FOUR

P ippa, Jordy, Ezra, and I returned to our suites after dinner.

"I think we're going to go out dancing tonight," Pippa said as Jordy unlocked their door. "You and Ezra should join us."

"No, you and Jordy go and enjoy yourselves," I told her. "I think Ezra and I are just going to go watch the sunset from the back deck, then maybe take a walk later on tonight. Just decompress a little bit after the full day of travel."

"That sounds nice too," Pippa told me, "but a whole week without JayJay and J.P.? Jordy and I are going to enjoy every second of it. Besides, my man's got some nice hip action on the dance floor." She grinned and pinched his butt.

Jordy gave her a look that was full of heat. "Not just on the dance floor," he said.

"TMI," I told them with a laugh. "Well, you two do

you. If we get a wild hair, we'll join you at the club later tonight."

After Pippa and Jordy entered their room, I knocked on Gilly's door. I was surprised when she answered.

"Hey," I said. "I just wanted to check on you, see how you were doing."

"I'm feeling a lot better," she said. "Scott ordered me some chicken noodle soup, and I was able to keep it down. So, yay — progress."

"Oh, good. That's really good news. Ezra and I are getting ready to clean up and go watch the sunset out on the back deck. Maybe take a walk later on if you guys want to join us."

"I'm not sure I'm up for a walk on this big moving ship tonight," she admitted. "But we'll happily watch the sunset with you guys."

I gave Gilly a quick hug. "See you on the balcony."

We were lucky that our rooms were facing west on our way to Cozumel. It meant we had a front-row seat to the gorgeous sunset.

I flossed, brushed my teeth, and changed into less formal, stretchy, wide-leg pants and a cotton scoop-neck shirt. Ezra put on a pair of cargo shorts and a pale-yellow t-shirt. His legs were nicely muscled, but they hadn't seen the sun since August. They were so, so white.

"Nice mayonnaise legs," I teased.

"You like them?" He turned his ankle out like a model showing off a new shoe. "I hear they're all the rage with the Gen Zs."

"I'm sure Mason, Ari, and Marco would have something to say about it." I snickered.

Mason, Ari, and Marco were all in college now, living their best lives. Mason, Ezra's son, was still doing fantastic at the University of Missouri. He finished his bachelor's in biomedical science and had already started the master's program for Biomedical Research. He'd applied for a Teacher Assistant job in the department and got it, which meant his tuition was paid, and he received a stipend every semester for teaching two biology classes to first-year students.

Gilly's twins were doing terrific as well. Marco, who'd been playing baseball at a local community college, had gotten scouted by Central University. He was offered a full-ride scholarship to play for two more years there. He talked it over with Gilly, and within a few days, he was signing the paperwork. Ari was killing it at Sanderson Institute of Technology, and she was already being courted by several big tech companies, along with NASA.

Watching Ezra's son and my godchildren turn into amazing adults was so much fun.

"Let's not ask them and say we did," Ezra said. "I'm not sure my ego can take their shade."

"Probably for the best." I rose up on my toes and kissed him. "Let's go see if the show is worth the price of admission."

It definitely was.

We sat in the chairs on the balcony, holding hands, feet propped up on the rail. The water below shimmered, reflecting the tangerine and vermillion streaks that painted the sky. The ocean looked like it had been dipped in molten gold, rippling with every gentle wave.

When it was over, I felt like I'd taken a Valium.

"That was so beautiful." The tension in my neck and back had magically disappeared. The ocean was a prescription I hadn't known I needed. "I haven't been this relaxed in years."

"Same." Ezra agreed, helping me up from the chair. "There's something about being out of cell phone range of all your problems. It's like the sea is giving us permission to just let it all go."

"That's how I feel." I slid my arms around him. "We should make this a yearly occurrence. Get away to somewhere we're not tied to our lives."

"I vote yes," he said.

"Me too," Gilly called over from her balcony. "Only, next time, maybe we do an all-inclusive resort instead of a giant rocking cradle."

"We can look into that, too." I looked over at her and smiled. "Ezra and I are going to go up to the lido deck and stretch our legs. Are you sure you don't want to come?"

"Scott can go if he wants," she said guiltily. "I hate that he's been stuck in the room with me."

"I'm not leaving you," he affirmed from behind her. "We have the rest of the week to explore."

"It's settled then." Gilly waved us off. "Have fun. I'm going to make it an early night, so I'll see you in the morning."

We said our goodnights, then made our way to the elevator and up to explore the upper decks.

———

STRETCHING our legs had involved walking the perimeter of the pool deck for an hour, sipping piña coladas from one of the bars for another hour, and then hitting the casino, where I lost twenty dollars on a quarter slot, and Ezra won it back on a nickel machine. By that time, it was after ten o'clock.

"You showed those slots who's the boss. My hero." I linked my arm with his. "That was fun. I haven't been in a casino since nineteen ninety-four when my work sent me to Vegas for a beauty convention."

"Hmmm," Ezra mused. "In nineteen ninety-four, I was—"

I gave him a kiss to shut him up. "I have no interest in knowing what kind of diaper you wore as a toddler."

He chuckled. "I wasn't a toddler."

"Close enough." I gave him a nudge with my elbow. I was getting tired, but I wasn't quite ready to put a lid on the evening. "Let's go up to the spa deck. I bet it's deserted at this time of night." I laughed as a notion popped into my head. "Maybe we can find a nook and cranny where you can explore my nooks and crannies."

He picked up the pace at the suggestion, making me laugh even more. God, I loved that man.

The Resplendent Retreat was an amenity for people in the concierge-class rooms and above, so we had to use our card key to get past the gate. Two women exited the hot tub when we got to the spa area. They wrapped towels around themselves, then holding hands, they walked past us toward the gate.

The area was quiet and peaceful. The soft glow of lantern-style lights lined the walkways, and the sound of trickling water came from the hydrotherapy pool. The briny sea air mixed with herbal scents of eucalyptus and lavender.

It felt like a hidden sanctuary, a world away from the bustling pool deck below.

The steam coming off the hot tub curled into the air and disappeared into the night sky. After a long day, a hot soak sounded divine.

"Now I wish we'd have brought our swimming trunks."

"We could always skinny dip."

"Hah!" I shook my head. "You're hilarious. God knows how many cameras they have up on this deck. My clothes are staying on."

"It'll be harder to explore your nooks and crannies that way, but I'm up for the challenge." He wrapped his arm around my waist and pulled me into an embrace. The heat from the hot tub was no match for the sizzle of his lips on mine.

There was a narrow passage on the other side of the towel rack that was dark and hidden. Perfect for a bit of privacy. I dragged Ezra into the shadow, gasping as he sandwiched me between his body and the wall, one arm around my back while his free hand slid under my shirt and up my waist. The warmth of his mouth on my neck raised goosebumps on my flesh.

"Yes," I rasped, as he explored even more.

The sound of a chair or something metal scraping across the deck brought our tête-à-tête to a screeching halt. My eyes widened at Ezra. It was dark, but my vision had adjusted enough that I could see him put his finger to his lips, then point down south. His cargo pants were doing a poor job of hiding his arousal.

Stepping out of the shadows now wasn't an option. We'd have to wait it out.

I nodded, trying not to giggle at the absurdity. There was a splash, then another splash.

I raised my brows at Ezra. He shrugged, then side-stepped to the end of the passage and peeked out. He looked at me and shook his head. "I can't see anyone," he whispered.

We heard the scraping sound again. "What in the world is going on?" I whispered.

We both leaned a little closer to the edge of the wall, peeking around the corner.

We didn't see anyone when we stepped out, but then I noticed something dark floating on the surface of the hydrotherapy pool.

"Ezra," I said, my voice uneasy. "It looks like someone threw something in the pool. Is that someone's clothes?"

His expression tightened as we crossed the deck to the bubbling water. "Someone in their clothes," he said.

Oh, no. There was a body in the pool, face down in the water.

Ezra, trained for moments like this, didn't hesitate. He jumped into the water, cutting through it with quick, powerful strokes. He reached the body in seconds and maneuvered the man toward the edge. I dropped to my knees, heart racing, and helped pull him onto the deck.

"Oh, no," I breathed, as I turned the man onto his back. "It's Sebastian Caldwell."

His spray-tanned skin was sallow, and his body limp. He wasn't breathing. I pressed my fingers to his neck, searching for a pulse. Nothing.

"No pulse or respiration," I said, my voice shaking.

"I'll start CPR," Ezra said immediately. His voice was steady, but his face wasn't. "I saw a red phone on the other side of the hot tub. Call the medical clinic. Tell them it's an emergency."

Adrenaline propelled me to my feet. I ran to the phone and grabbed it, my hands shaking as I punched in *111*, the number listed for the clinic.

"You've reached the medical center on deck two. This is Nurse Tony," a man answered. He sounded bored as if he were expecting someone complaining about seasickness or a headache. "What can I help you with tonight?"

"We pulled a man out of the hydrotherapy pool in the Resplendent Retreat," I blurted. "He's not breathing, and I couldn't find a pulse. My partner's doing CPR."

The boredom disappeared from his voice. "I'm on my way."

"Please, hurry." I hung up the phone and raced back to Ezra, who hadn't missed a beat with the compressions. "A nurse is coming," I told him, breathless. "Anything?"

Ezra didn't look up. His face was tight with focus, his hands moving steadily. "Nothing yet," he said through gritted teeth. "Come on, buddy. Breathe."

Sebastian's skin looked waxy under the deck lights, his dark hair plastered to his forehead. Water pooled around him as it drained from his clothes. The wine stain on his shirt from dinner was faded, but still there.

My throat burned. "Come on, you jerk," I whispered. "Don't do this."

Ezra tilted Sebastian's head back and gave him two rescue breaths.

I heard footfalls from behind the bar area moving quickly toward us. I turned as a man in a white uniform appeared, a medical bag slung over his shoulder.

"I'm Tony," he said, his voice brisk and professional. He dropped to his knees across from Ezra. "What do we have?"

"Found him face down in the hydrotherapy pool. No pulse, no breathing. We pulled him out and started CPR," Ezra said, not stopping. "I've been doing it for a few minutes now.

Tony nodded, already getting to work. He pulled a stethoscope and a small device from his bag, pressing it to Sebastian's chest. His jaw tightened. "No heartbeat." He glanced at me. "Did either of you see what happened?"

"No," I said, my voice dry and shaky. "We came up to

the spa deck, and then a minute or two later he was just... there. We didn't see anyone else."

Tony grabbed a portable defibrillator from his bag and cut open Sebastian's shirt.

"Okay, let's shock him." He placed the pads carefully on Sebastian's chest. "Clear."

Ezra leaned back, hands up.

The machine gave a high-pitched whine, then a sharp jolt. Sebastian's body twitched violently.

I held my breath.

"No rhythm." Tony reset the machine. "Clear."

Another jolt. Again, it failed to get Sebastian's heart started.

He did it twice more at increasing intensities, only to get the same outcome. Nothing. Tony sat back on his heels and shook his head, his expression grim. "I'm afraid it's too late. He's gone."

The world seemed to tilt. My knees wobbled. I pressed a hand to my chest, only then realizing I'd been holding my breath.

The nurse looked at me, his voice softer now. "Do either of you know this man?"

I swallowed hard and nodded. "Yes. He's in the suite next to ours with his wife. His name's Sebastian Caldwell."

Tony's brows lifted slightly, recognition flickering in his eyes. "The singing contest judge?"

"Yeah. That's him."

He looked anxious as he closed the defibrillator case. "That's not good."

I couldn't agree with him more. It certainly wasn't good for Sebastian.

The nurse's expression darkened. "Did you see what happened?"

"No." My fingers felt numb, so I curled them into fists to get the feeling back. "We heard some scraping, then a splash, then another splash, and more scraping. By the time we got to the pool, he was already in the water."

Tony exhaled sharply, his jaw tight. "Terrible accident," he said, but his eyes weren't convinced. "I'll notify the captain and security, too. You'll need to stick around and give them your statements."

Ezra stood slowly, his wet shorts dripping. His shoulders were tense, his jaw clenched so hard a muscle ticked near his temple.

I stepped closer to him, lowering my voice. "Ezra... what are you thinking?"

He didn't answer right away. He stared at Sebastian's still body for a moment longer, then exhaled slowly. His voice was low, edged with something cold and certain. "This wasn't an accident."

Unfortunately, I couldn't disagree. The metal scraping sound happened after the splashes. After Sebastian was in the water. Which meant, someone had been up here with him when he'd gone in, and...they'd left him to die.

## CHAPTER
# FIVE

The observation deck was quiet. The hydrotherapy pool where Sebastian's body had been pulled from had been turned off, and the water was eerily calm. Captain Steven Klein, a man in his fifties with a stocky build, stood a few feet away. His white uniform was immaculate, with gold and black epaulets squared on his shoulders. His matching white hat with a black bill low over his eyes gave him an authoritative air. Beside him, Security Chief Rebecca Hansen, slim, sharp-eyed, late thirties or maybe early forties, also dressed in a white uniform, talked in low tones with Dr. Nick Patel, the ship's doctor, and Nurse Tony. Patel looked like he was in his forties as well. He was tall, had dark hair, and had a serious expression. They kept their voices low, deliberately out of earshot from Ezra and me.

I shifted my weight, glancing at Ezra, who'd been given a terrycloth robe to cover his wet clothes. "What do you think they're saying?"

He sighed, rubbing a hand down his face. "A whole lot of CYA, if I had to guess." His voice was low and tired.

CYA was short for "Cover Your Ass." I'd been in plenty of meetings when I worked for a corporation where people would spend their entire time figuring out ways to make sure if crap hit the fan, it wouldn't fly back at them.

My gaze drifted back to Sebastian's body, now hidden under a white sheet. My thoughts went to Callie. She'd lost her first husband under strange circumstances, and now her second had died just as mysteriously. Bad luck or something worse? I didn't want to say it, but the word *black widow* lingered in my head.

Not my problem, though. We were off duty. This was supposed to be a vacation. No investigations, no dead bodies.

"I'm sure they'll figure it out," I said, though the way Tony had called it an accident too fast didn't sit right with me. Chief Hansen didn't look too convinced, either. Her arms were crossed, brows drawn tight as the group talked. She didn't look happy.

When their huddle finally broke, Hansen came over to us. "Could you describe what happened again? And where were you when the drowning took place?" Her voice was calm but firm. "Walk me through it again. From the start."

Ezra glanced at me, then nodded. He kept his voice even. "We were by the towel racks, on the other side of the hot tubs."

Hansen tilted her head. "What were you doing there?"

Ezra's jaw tensed. "We were... occupied."

"We were making out," I said bluntly. "That's not really the important part, though."

Her expression didn't change. "Go on."

I took a breath. "We heard this scraping sound first. It sounded like someone dragging a metal chair, or something like that. It was loud enough that we stopped what we were doing."

"Then we heard a splash," Ezra added. "A second one, right after the first."

"And more scraping after that," I finished. "It wasn't quiet, and it wasn't subtle. That's when we stepped out of the corridor to see what was happening."

"What did you see?" Hansen asked, her pen hovering over the page.

"Sebastian was already in the pool," Ezra said. His voice had gone tight. "Face down. He wasn't moving."

Hansen nodded slowly, jotting it all down. Her eyes flicked back up to us. "And you're sure about the order of the sounds? Scraping, splash, splash, then more scraping?"

I didn't hesitate. "Yes. I'm sure."

"Positive," Ezra backed me up.

Her eyes lingered on us for a second longer, like she was trying to read between the lines. Then she nodded again. "Okay. Got it." Chief Hansen's eyes stayed locked on me, her expression unreadable but her tone just a little too careful. "You're sure about the order of the sounds?" she asked again. "Scraping, then a splash, another splash, more scraping? Are you completely certain it wasn't the other way around? Scraping, scraping, splash, splash?"

I didn't waver, but I was becoming exasperated. "I'm sure. That's how it happened."

Her head tilted slightly. "Stress can play tricks on memory, especially when you're, uhm, distracted." Her gaze flicked between me and Ezra.

I exhaled slowly, keeping my voice even. "We weren't that distracted. I know what I heard."

Ezra leaned in a little, voice low and steady. "We're sure."

She studied us for a second longer, then tried again. "Are you positive? Sometimes—"

"I'm a special investigator with Garden Cove PD," Ezra cut in, his voice sharper now. "I've worked undercover with an FBI task force. Nora has worked as a consultant for the police department on multiple homicide cases. Trust me, we both know how to recall a scene under stress. We're sure."

"Can't you just look at your CCTV footage? You can verify our statements with your own eyes." While I hadn't seen any security cameras, I had little doubt they were there.

Her eyebrows lifted, clearly surprised. The cool, composed look flickered, just for a second. Then she nodded stiffly. Without another word, she turned and strolled back to the captain and the others. Their quiet huddle started up again.

We waited, silent, while they whispered and glanced our way more than once. It felt like forever before they finally broke apart.

Chief Hansen returned to us, her expression more neutral this time. "Thank you both for your patience. You can go back to your cabin now. If we need anything else, I'll find you."

"What about the investigation?" Ezra asked, his voice low but pointed.

"Don't worry, Mr. Holden," she said. "We'll do a thorough investigation. And after the doctor examines the body, we'll determine whether the drowning was an accident or not. But that's for us to handle, not you. You and Ms. Black should go back to enjoying your vacation."

"What will happen to Sebastian's body?" I asked, hoping they had a freezer somewhere that wasn't in one of the kitchens.

"We'll be moving it to the morgue," she said.

I frowned. "I've studied the deck plans for Lady Voyager, and I would've noticed a room marked as a morgue."

"It's on the bottom deck behind the medical center." Her voice hushed. "It's not something cruise lines like to advertise."

"How often do people die on cruises?" Ezra asked with incredulity.

"It's more common than I'd like to admit." She pivoted her gaze to the covered body. "This is my fourth since I was hired as the security chief two years ago."

I blew out a breath. "Yikes."

Hansen shrugged. "Accidents happen on a floating island, especially when you add alcohol to the mix."

"So," I said suspiciously. "They've all been accidents?"

"Yep," she replied quickly without elaborating.

"What about the body?" Ezra asked. "Will it stay on the ship until we get back to Tampa?"

"No." The security chief looked over her shoulder at the other crew members and then back to us. "Once we inform any family members onboard, we'll help them make arrangements to disembark at our first port of call to repatriate their loved one home."

Sebastian was British. Did that mean he would go back to the UK or the states?

"Operation Rising Star," I heard Tony's voice through Hansen's radio. "Keep the aft service elevator clear for the next hour."

"Copy that," a crackling voice came back.

"Operation Rising Star?" I mean, Sebastian was a star-maker, but it seemed a little on the nose.

"It's our code for when we're transporting a body."

"Interesting."

The captain legged it over to us. "Well, folks, I'm sure this wasn't part of your itinerary, and I apologize for any inconvenience this tragedy has caused." He gave us a tight, but genial smile. "We'd certainly appreciate your discretion in this matter," he added smoothly. "You understand, I'm sure." His voice was polite, but the message was clear. "A death on board can be... disruptive. Talk to Natalie Carmine, our director of guest services, in the morning. Tell Nat that you're special friends of Captain Steve. She'll take care of any spa and salon treatments you need to help you relax back into your vacation...on the house, of course."

A payoff to keep us quiet. Classy.

"Thank you, Captain Steve," I said, keeping my voice level. "If there's nothing else, we'd like to leave."

"Of course," he said, nodding solemnly. "I can't imagine how traumatic tonight must have been for you. If there's anything you need, let me know. If I can't help you personally, I'll find someone on the ship who can. When you're on the *Lady Voyager*, you're always in good hands."

Too bad Sebastian Caldwell hadn't been.

Ezra, with barely a nod toward the captain and crew, took my hand and led me away without another word. We walked in silence, past a long row of deserted lounge chairs, out the privacy gate, and to the nearest elevator. The panel dinged softly when the elevator arrived, the doors sliding open.

Once inside, the doors shut, and Ezra let out a low, frustrated growl. "That was not an accident."

"Agreed," I said. "I'm not even sure it was a drowning."

"Mmm-hmm." He rubbed his thumb against my palm. "I have my doubts as well. He wasn't in the water for more than a minute before we got him out."

"Yeah, that feels farfetched." Besides, someone else had been in the spa area. I was certain of it. Even so, it wasn't like we could do anything. We were in international waters, and the captain decided whether to bring in outside law enforcement. And even if we weren't in international waters, getting the FBI to chopper in to take over the investigation was even more farfetched. "This isn't Garden Cove. It's not our case."

"Nope," Ezra said. "Not our town. Not our problem to solve."

"Although, since his wife's in the cabin next to ours, it would be positively rude not to check in on her."

"It would be downright unfriendly."

"After she's been informed, of course."

"Of course," he conceded.

"And maybe, while we're being neighborly, we could ask a couple of easy, not-too-invasive questions about what Sebastian was doing after dinner."

Ezra squeezed my hand. "Nothing wrong with some non-invasive inquiries."

"And if she invites us inside their suite, and my aroma mojo happens to kick in?" I put up a hand. "Well, I can't help it if any visions I might get give us some insight, right?"

Ezra chuckled, the tension in him finally breaking. "God, I love you."

I grinned, smug with pleasure that I'd shifted his mood. "So... a little sun, a little fun, and a dab of investigation?"

He dipped his face to mine and kissed me. "Sounds like a plan."

CHAPTER

# SIX

Ezra and I returned to our room. We made the decision to save the news of what happened to Sebastian until morning. It was late, and no doubt Gilly, Scott, Jordy, and Pippa were already down for the night. After crawling into our comfortable bed, sleep hit us fast and hard. We were out like the lights in seconds, not minutes.

The following morning, we gathered everyone in Pippa and Jordy's room. The walls were paper thin, but their room was the farthest from the new widow's. It felt safer to discuss her husband's death there than in our room. Coffee was passed around while Ezra and I filled the group in on everything from the night before.

"We see a few drownings every year in the emergency room," Scott said. "It's possible to drown that quickly, but since you administered CPR right away, I'm skeptical he was alive when he went into the pool," Scott said, leaning forward with his elbows on his knees. "I'd love to get my eyes on the doctor's medical findings to see if there was actually any water in the lungs."

Gilly, looking much better than she had the night before, shook her head as she gave me the stink eye. "Why am I even surprised that if there's a dead body on our vacation, you're the one to stumble over it?"

She aimed that at me, but Ezra spoke first. "More like the dead body stumbled over us."

"Okay," Pippa said, her voice brisk and no-nonsense. "Let's say we're running with the idea that someone else was at the Resplendent last night. Someone dragged the body onto that chair or something like it. Who, though? And how did they get him to the top deck without anyone noticing? Did they have an access card? Wouldn't their room number register when they swiped it?"

"All good questions with no good answers," I said. "The obvious suspect is Callie, the wife. This is her second husband to die. She's either got awful luck, or she's involved. Then there's Charise, our clumsy steward."

"Oh!" Pippa grabbed her phone from the coffee table. "I downloaded this video at the wifi bar last night." She tapped the screen and pulled up the clip.

Our steward Charise, her hair longer when she was on the show, appeared on stage wearing a sparkling red dress and matching glittery blue heels. She belted out a lyrical and haunting rendition of *The Star-Spangled Banner* as if she belonged on a Broadway stage. Her high notes soared, and her low notes were rich and powerful.

"She sounds terrific," Gilly said. "Her voice is amazing."

*The camera shifted to the judges. Sebastian sat in the middle, not just unimpressed but bored out of his mind. Charise's expression changed as she noticed his lack of enthusiasm. When Sebastian glanced down at his phone mid-song, her expression fell even more. Next, he yawned as she sang a run, and that was it. Her voice cracked on the final, powerful note.*

"That was so rude," Scott said, wincing.

"That's not even the worst part," Pippa said. "Wait for it."

*The first judge, who I recognized as Emerson Lake, an R&B singer from the seventies, leaned forward, smiling warmly. "Charise, your voice is stunning. You've got something really special. Your raw, emotional tone gave me chills." He splayed his hands. "But I noticed you holding back a little. Trust yourself, child, you got this."*

*The second judge, Molly Damsel, a pop diva from the eighties, nodded eagerly. "I agree with Emerson. In the beginning, you connected with the song beautifully, and that's rare. But as the song went on, I could see your confidence waver, especially on the big notes." She smiled at Charise. "That's okay. It happens to the best of us. It's something you can work on. When you let go of all that fear, you're going to be unstoppable."*

*Charise fidgeted with the microphone, nodding. "Thank you, Molly."*

*"You're great, you're great," Molly repeated as she leaned*

*back in her seat. "Sebastian," she said. "What did you think of Charise's performance."*

*And then it was Sebastian's turn to speak.*

*He made a show of looking down at the table before dragging his eyes up to Charise. "Total, one hundred percent dreadful. It makes me wonder if you two were in the same room as me." He turned his words to Charise. "Your voice is a six out of ten, but your stage presence is a zero. It was about as bad as it gets. I don't know why you've had any encouragement whatsoever."*

*"Come on, Sebastian," Molly said. "She wasn't that bad."*

*"She wasn't good either." He gestured toward Charise, who looked like she'd been slapped. "Whatever the opposite of entertaining is, that was you. Pathetic."*

*The host stepped in, placing a hand on Charise's back. "Is there anything you'd like to say to the judges?"*

*"I...I...I've been taking vocal lessons since I was five," she managed, her voice shaking. "I know I can sing circles around the other contestants. If you give me another chance, I'll prove it. I'm a fighter."*

*Sebastian scoffed. "From what I just witnessed, you couldn't fight your way out of a paper chippie cone. As for your vocal instructor, what he's taught you is criminal. He should be blindfolded and made to listen to you sing while a firing squad takes aim."*

*"That's not fair," Charise said, her voice breaking as tears fell. "I—"*

*"If you want to be rude because you can't handle constructive criticism, you can leave the stage."*

*"But—"*

*"I said, leave."*

The video cut off as she ran offstage.

"Holy cow." My chest felt tight with secondhand embarrassment. "That was the most brutal thing I've ever seen, and I've had visions of murder. He verbally eviscerated her."

"Yep," Pippa said. "That's why I recognized her last night. She was the first person voted out of the top ten that season. I've seen him say some mean stuff to contestants, but nothing like that. After that episode, his critiques were more gentle, mixing good with the bad. I'm pretty sure a producer had taken him to task about crossing the line from smart-mouthed mean-girl into hateful bully territory."

"She made it all the way to the top ten just to be treated like that?" Gilly's hands curled into fists. "I'm not sad he's dead, if I'm being honest."

I couldn't blame her. I barely knew the man, but after watching that, I wanted revenge for Charise too.

"There were worse singers in the top ten," Pippa said. "But he seemed to have a real bee up his butt about Charise."

I nodded. "After seeing that, I'd say she's definitely at the top of the suspect list."

"Do you think Callie's been informed yet?" Scott asked.

"I'm sure they told her last night," I said. "But I didn't hear anything from her room." I glanced at Ezra. "Did you?"

He shook his head. "Nothing."

"Hmm." I sipped my coffee. "I'm sure they've found her by now."

"Well, we can't do anything about it right now," Gilly said with a sigh. "So, I vote we go get breakfast. After that, I want to hit the sun deck, catch some rays, and read."

"And the murder?" Pippa asked, raising a brow.

"If it is a murder," Gilly said, playing devil's advocate, "let's leave it to the professionals."

Ezra shot her a dry look.

She wiggled her fingers at him. "You know what I mean. Ship security professionals."

"And if they try to cover it up and call it an accident?" I asked.

"If that happens, you have my permission to ruin your first real vacation in years," Gilly said. "Until then, leave it alone. Okay?"

I didn't want to argue, so I nodded. Ezra caught my eye, his brows slightly raised. I gave a small shake of my head.

Good. He was still with me, and I was with him. Gilly hadn't found Sebastian. She didn't do CPR or watch him get shocked again and again with no result. She hadn't heard the second person on the deck. She wasn't invested the way Ezra and I were.

"Okay," I said finally. "Let's get breakfast and see where the day takes us."

***

THERE WAS a consensus to eat breakfast in the main dining room, where we'd had dinner the night before. The breakfast cooked to order sounded delicious, and I was in the mood for some over-medium fried eggs, bacon, and crispy hash browns. The chances were slim to none that Charise would work both breakfast and dinner shifts, but I'll admit that was partially the reason for my vote.

"I'm having the avocado toast with the poached egg," Pippa said with enthusiasm.

"How millennial of you," I teased.

She rolled her eyes. "I'm practically Gen X."

Gilly snorted a laugh. "Pippa, sweetheart, I love you like I love my left foot, but in no way, shape, or form are you practically Gen X."

She lifted her hands and began lowering fingers one at a time. "My parents neglected me. I was left to fend for myself before and after school…" She paused, seemingly stumped.

"Go on," Gilly told her. "I'll wait."

Pippa put her hands down. "It's too early in the morning to think this hard."

"All right, Nora. Let's show her how it's done." Gilly held up both hands.

"Latchkey kid," I said.

Gilly put a finger down.

"Nuclear hot metal slides that burned the skin off your thighs."

She put another finger down.

"Trash eighties."

Gilly laughed again and put her next finger down.

Pippa's brow dipped. "What's a trash eighties?"

"I'm glad you asked," Ezra muttered.

"It was the TRS-80 computers we had in school. This was before the internet. We had DOS-based computers that you could program. I made a program that would find the sine, cosine, or tangent of an equation as long as you knew two of the numbers. I used it to cheat in math."

Gilly snickered. "I programmed Pixel Dog to walk across the bottom of the screen."

Scott chuckled. "That's my girl."

"I'm sorry I asked," Pippa said with a sigh. "To stop you from going on and on, I'll concede that I'm not Gen X."

"Awww." I stuck my lower lip out in a pout. "We'll let you have Xennial if it will make you feel better." Even if she was a few years away from her forties.

"It will make me feel better," she said brightly.

Our conversation going to the dining room was easy and breezy. Literally. The wind was crazy on the open part of the deck you had to pass to get to the restaurants.

When we got to the main dining area, Gilly whistled. "This place is huge."

It wasn't decorated as fancy as it had been for dinner, but the sea maiden was still dumping water over her head.

"Stay away from open flames and the fountain," Scott warned, and we all laughed again. On their first date, Gilly tripped into a flambé, her dress caught on fire, and Scott tackled her into a koi fountain to put her out.

Her dress, unfortunately, became see-through when wet, and everyone got a good look at her fancy red underwear and bra. The thought of that night, even with the dead body, made me smile.

"I won't order any flaming desserts," she promised.

The hostess told us it was open seating, so we picked a table near the fountain. That's when I saw the security chief, Rebecca Hansen, just outside the entrance. I tapped Ezra's leg and used my chin to gesture in her direction.

"Come on," he said, getting up.

"Where are you going?" Gilly asked.

"We'll be right back," I told her. "If the server comes around before we do, order me a coffee and some orange juice."

"Gotcha covered." She gave me a thumbs-up. "What about you, Easy?"

"I'm coffeed out," he said. "I'll take some ice water, though."

We made a quick beeline to the entrance, worried Hansen would leave before we could catch her. When she saw us coming, I could tell she was debating whether or not to make a run for it. Lucky for us, she stayed put.

"Good morning, Mr. Holden and Ms. Black. Can I help you with something?" she asked.

I came right out with my first question. "Did you look at the video footage from the spa area?"

"I can't comment on an open investigation. With what you told me about your experience with police work, you should know that."

I tried to keep the irritation out of my voice. My mother always said you catch more flies with honey than vinegar. "So, you did see the second person on the video," I said. "I don't understand why you can't just say it. It only confirms what we told you."

"There's no video," she blurted before snapping her mouth shut. "I shouldn't have told you that."

"What do you mean no video?" Ezra asked suspiciously. "You probably have a dozen cameras up there."

We hadn't noticed any, but it stood to reason.

"We have two. One pointed at the hydrotherapy pool area and one by the bar. It's an exclusive area, and our guests pay for privacy, so we don't put cameras on the hot tubs, the steam room, or in any of the shower or bathroom areas."

"You said you have one on the pool," he poked. "I don't understand the problem."

"And it's not your problem to understand," she gritted out between her teeth in a hushed voice. "But, if you must know, there was evidence of rodents near the camera's mount, and the wiring in the back had been chewed through. There is no video."

I crossed my arms over my chest. "Isn't that convenient."

Hansen gave me a chastising glance. "There's not a single thing convenient about it, Ms. Black. Now, if you'll excuse me, I have to get back to work."

"Hey," I said before she could get away. "Did you inform Callie Caldwell about her husband's death yet?" Before she could lecture me on open investigations again, I added, "She's my neighbor. I don't want to say the wrong thing if I run into her."

Hansen sighed, then nodded. "Not yet," she told us. "She wasn't in her cabin last night." My face must've registered alarm because the security chief continued. "We have a few all-night activities open, like the casino and such. I'm getting ready to go to her suite now and try again."

"I'd ask if you'll keep us informed," Ezra told her, "but I'm pretty sure I know the answer."

"Now we're starting to understand each other," Hansen said. "If I require anything more from the two of you, I'll come find you." She whipped around on her heel and speed-walked away.

I looked at Ezra. "Did you buy that about the rat?"

"Oh, I definitely think there's a rat," he said. "But the kind that moves on two legs, not four."

Speaking of rats, where was Callie? Her scarcity kept her at the top of the suspect board, and it would take overwhelming evidence and a strong alibi to change my mind.

# CHAPTER
# SEVEN

$S$ cott and Jordy talked Ezra into teeing off for eighteen rounds on the golf simulator on deck twelve. That left Gilly, Pippa, and me to our own devices, and I had a few ideas of my own on how we should spend the rest of our morning."

"How would you ladies like a spa treatment?" I asked my two besties. "It's on Captain Steve." I'd told them about the captain's bribe to keep me quiet. Well, a sixty-minute massage and a facial would keep me quiet for at least two hours.

Gilly looked uncertain. "I'm not sure that invitation extends past you. I don't want it to get awkward."

Gilly was a board-certified licensed masseuse, and she offered her clients a wide variety of massages, including sports, chakra, deep tissue, stone, trigger point, and, recently, she'd trained in oncology massage. When she told me she was doing it, I'd gotten emotional.

My mother had died from cancer. It was such a terrible illness, and that she had trained to bring comfort to people who were in constant pain...well, it made me love my BFF even more. I already loved her to infinity and back, so loving her more achieved the impossible. On top of that, she offered the massages for free to the people in our community who were battling the disease. If they were handing out sainthoods at the pearly gates, I had a feeling there was a badge up there waiting for Gilly to pick up.

"I won't hear another word on the matter," I told her in a tone that brook no argument. "The captain wanted me to relax and get back to enjoying my vacation, and I can't do that without the two of you."

Pippa giggled. "I'll take a free spa treatment. I've been meaning to get a facial for two months and haven't had the time."

"Then I think it's time we went and found Natalie Carmine, and get the VIP treatment."

Guest services was on deck four, and I asked for directions after we meandered for about ten minutes without finding it. It turned out that it was just several desks lined up in an alcove behind the photo villa and Wi-Fi lounge. Four women and two men in blue pants and white shirts helped guests book shore excursions, salon and spa appointments, and dinner reservations at the specialty restaurants on the fifth floor.

There was a leggy blonde with a nighttime amount of makeup on her face standing over a podium as she flipped the pages of what looked like a ledger. I was going to ask her if she knew where we could find Natalie, but I had to look no further.

"Hello," I said, trying not to startle her.

She looked up, nonplussed. "Hello," she greeted back. "Can I help you?"

Suddenly, I felt a little jittery. I'd been confident when I assured Pippa and Gilly I could get us all a free spa day, but uncertainty reared its ugly head. "Captain Steve told me to find you today. He said to say I was a special friend, and you'd book me...uhm, and my friends, some spa treatments, on him.

The corner of her mouth tugged up into a half smile. Close up, I could see she overlined her lips to give them a fuller, more sensuous look. It totally worked at a distance, but the illusion didn't hold from a foot or two away. Still, she was an attractive woman, and she had an air of confidence and authority.

"Any friend of Captain Steve's is a friend of mine," she said genially. "I'm more than happy to get your treatments booked. Do you want to look over the spa menu for a moment? Or do you know what you want?"

"I'd love to look at a menu," Pippa told her.

"Same," Gilly added.

I shrugged at her. "I guess we'll look at menus."

"Excellent." Natalie's smile was warm and genuine. She'd either perfected the art of looking happy to people, or she was actually happy to see people. Either way, her demeanor had put me back at ease. She opened a drawer in a nearby desk and took three velvety booklets with Serenity Spa embossed on the front and handed them to us. "Here you go," she said. "Why don't you three have a seat on the couch over there. Take your time, and when you know what you want, just wave me over, and I'll get you set up."

We sat down together, our knees touching as we huddled over our menus.

"That was easier than I thought it would be," Gilly muttered out of the side of her mouth.

"I know," I muttered back. "Being Captain Steve's special friend has its privileges."

"Better than a platinum card," Pippa agreed.

"We should book some dinner reservations for the week. Scott and I want to try the Brazilian restaurant, and doesn't Jordy want to eat at that Japanese place?" Gilly asked. "Nora, is there any place you and Ezra have a hankerin' for?"

"For dinner?" I shook my head. "We're good with whatever, but they have a taqueria on board that I heard made the best street tacos. You know I could eat those breakfast, lunch, and dinner."

"You really do love a taco journey," Gilly lamented.

"Hey," I said with all sincerity. "I can't please everyone. I'm not a taco."

Pippa choked on a laugh. "We'll get lunch there today."

"And maybe tomorrow....and the next day."

"Tomorrow, we'll be in Cozumel," Pippa gushed. "I

can't wait to snorkel with turtles." Her body was rigid as she tried to contain her excitement. "I hope my camera works. I bought one of those cheap waterproof ones online."

"Did you test it out?" Gilly asked.

"I put it in a bowl of water overnight, and it stayed dry. It takes decent pictures, too. Better than my phone."

"Scott and I are going to try our hand at a recreational dive. He's been talking non-stop about how if he enjoys it, he wants to get certified." Gilly smiled. "If it makes him happy, I'm all for it. And there are places to dive in the Midwest." She made a face. "They call it muck diving, which doesn't sound appetizing at all."

"It sounds mucky," I quipped, enjoying the moment with my pals. But Cozumel meant adventures for them. For me, it was the end of the road for Sebastian Caldwell. He would be disembarked, and there was a chance that if the captain officially determined his death and accident, we'd never know how he died or why. I wasn't sure why I cared. The man was a real piece of crap. The way he'd talked to his wife. Gah. I'd wanted to slap him. And hearing the way he'd gone after Charise, I was surprised someone hadn't killed him sooner.

But he was a human being, even if he was the worst kind of human being. If Callie was responsible, it was probably for a payday. I also wondered about her first husband. I mentally made a note to stop by the WiFi lounge next door and do an internet search and see what I could find out. Maybe I'd email Reese while I was at it. She was covering for Ezra this week at the station, and she was feeling pretty darn good about the temporary promotion. Maybe good enough to be inclined to do a little digging on an old case.

"Earth to Nora," Gilly said to get my attention. She sighed. Heavily. "You're thinking about Caldwell, aren't you?"

I hadn't told them about the security chief's inability to track down the widow and give her the news. "Callie wasn't in her suite last night," I informed them. "At least not when they tried to deliver the bad news."

"Where do you think she was?" Pippa asked.

Gilly gave her a flat look. "Murdering her husband, then hiding any evidence."

Pippa bumped her with her shoulder. "Smart aleck."

"I think we know that we're not going to get Nora's best until we help her put this mystery to bed, so..." She winked at me. "So, we'll help."

"Yay!" I squealed.

"Hey," Gilly complained. "I didn't agree to this."

I gave her my most pathetic sad face.

"Fine," she huffed. "I'll help too."

"Double yay!" Knowing I had their support put me at ease. I wasn't relishing the idea of lying to them about my whereabouts today. "Ezra and I made plans to do a little sleuthing after lunch."

Gilly chuckled. "You mean snooping."

"Potatoes, poh-tah-toes."

"Our help is on one condition, though," Gilly amended. "You have until we dock in Cozumel to do your aroma mojo thing and figure out the bad guy, but if we can't solve the mystery by then, you have to promise me you'll let it go and enjoy the rest of the trip. Once that body's off the boat, there's not a whole lot any of us can do about it."

"True." I sagged back on the couch. If the death was declared an accidental drowning, once Sebastian and Callie were in Cozumel, I would have no other choice than to let it go. "Fine," I conceded. "It's a deal."

Natalie must've gotten impatient because she approached with an open tablet in hand before we called her over. "Do you ladies know what treatments you'd like?"

"I'm going to take the Ambrosia package," I told her. It was a sea salt scrub, a sixty-minute Swedish massage, and finished with a thirty-minute facial.

"Oh, that sounds good," Gilly said. "Me too."

"Me three," Pippa added.

"And when would you like your treatments?" she asked.

I looked back and forth between both my girls, and they both nodded.

"Tuesday morning after breakfast, around ten a.m.," Gill said. "We'll start our next fun day at sea with a bang."

The guest services director frowned as she scrolled around on her tablet. "Is it okay if we stagger the three of you? It's the only way to get the three of you in close to the same time? I can get you in at nine-thirty, ten, and ten-thirty. That will get all of you out of there in time for a late lunch. I'll just need your names and room numbers, please."

We obliged.

"Thanks, Natalie." I got up from the couch, using my besties as leverage. "I appreciate it."

They got up after and stood on either side of me. "You're the best," Gilly told her.

"Let me know if you need anything else," she said as we were leaving.

"Where to?" Pippa asked once we were in the corridor and out of earshot of anyone.

"I think we need to go back up to the Resplendent Retreat. I need to see it in the light of day, and, who knows, maybe I'll be able to see something..." I touch my nose. "...that I couldn't see last night."

"I like it," Gilly said. "Let's do it."

"WiFi Lounge first," I told them. "I want to look up Callie's first husband's death, and email Reese to see if she can access the police database or call in a favor to see what exactly made the police suspect that the death was suspicious and why they couldn't get anything to stick in the investigation."

Pippa raised her hand. "You and Gilly check out the retreat. I'll do the computer legwork and email Reese. When we're done, we can meet at the taqueria and compare notes."

"Tacos!" I laughed, feeling lighter than I had all morning. I had my two closest allies giving me their full support, and it had been exactly what I needed. Since our phones were basically bricks on the ship, I'd worn a watch. The time as four minutes after eleven. "Okay. Let's meet in one hour, regardless of what we find."

Pippa and Gilly agreed, and we were off. Time wasn't our friend. We had until eight a.m. on Monday to get Sebastian's death figured out, or someone, maybe his wife, was going to literally get away with murder. I couldn't let that happen. Not if I could help it.

# EIGHT

Gilly and I left Pippa on the fourth floor and headed up to deck sixteen. I wasn't sure what I expected when we got to the gate. Maybe police tape or some kind of barrier cordoning off the Resplendent Retreat, but no. It looked like the death of a guest on their ship had been nothing more than a blip on the radar, and, today, it was business as usual.

We swiped our key cards and entered. Surprisingly, there were fewer than twenty people inside. Given that the area was reserved for concierge-level guests and those staying in the more extravagant suites, I understood why.

A sign in front of the hydrotherapy pool declared it **Closed for Maintenance**. It was the only indication that something terrible had happened here. If we hadn't found Sebastian's lifeless body floating in that very pool, we never would have known. We hadn't heard a whisper of rumors circulating the ship about a sudden death.

They had a tight-lipped crew. I wondered how many staff members had even been told about the incident.

"Well, at least they had the good sense to shut down the pool." Gilly planted her hands on her hips. "I can't tell you how angry I'd be if I found out I'd been swimming in the dead guy soup."

"Okay... gross." I grimaced. "I'm sure the filtration system handled... whatever bodily fluids or, uh, other things might have ended up in there." Still, I agreed with her. The thought made my stomach turn.

The same scent from the night before lingered in the air. Eucalyptus and lavender. It wasn't as strong now, but I picked up warm undertones of sandalwood and something sweeter, maybe jasmine or hibiscus with softer notes of vanilla. Or was that chocolate? I inhaled deeply, trying to discern the difference. It was chocolate. Nice. The aromatic blend smelled incredible. I made a mental note to experiment with the combination when I got home for a new soap and lotion line for the shop.

"Okay," Gilly said, her voice light but her eyes serious. "Where do we start? You point us in the right direction."

A young man in a crisp uniform walked by, balancing a tray of drinks. He delivered them to a couple lounging by the hot tubs. The badge on his shirt named him as Bruno.

"Excuse me?" I lifted my hand to get his attention when he was walking back to the bar with the empty tray.

He stopped, offering a polite, toothy smile. "Can I get

you ladies something to drink?" His accent was thick, though I couldn't quite place it, maybe Eastern European. Still, he spoke clearly enough for me to understand.

I gestured vaguely around us, circling my finger in the air. "Do you know what this scent is? It's amazing."

His grin widened. "That's our signature fragrance," he said proudly. "It's called *Resplendent Relaxation*."

"It's lovely," I told him sincerely.

He held up a hand in a gesture for us to wait. "One moment, ladies. I'll be right back."

He hurried over to the towel shack, stood on his toes to reach over the counter, and rummaged underneath. A moment later, he jogged back, holding out his hand.

"Here you go," he said, handing me a small stack of sealed packets, each the size of an alcohol wipe. "We have samples for guests. You can use them in your cabin."

I blinked in surprise, accepting the packets. "Thank you. That's really... thoughtful of you."

He gave a small nod. "The fragrance is sold in larger sizes at the Serenity Spa. You should get you a bottle so you can take the retreat anywhere you go."

"Thanks for the tip." I'd look into getting me a bottle when we went for our treatments on Tuesday.

His grin widened. "Now, can I get you ladies something to drink?"

"I'm good," I told him.

"I'll take a strawberry daiquiri," Gilly piped up.

I gave her a look, and she shrugged. "What? I'm just here for moral support. I don't have to be sober for that."

I chuckled despite myself. "Nope, I guess you don't."

Trying to seem casual, I wandered toward the hydrotherapy pool, Gilly at my side. I didn't want to draw attention. The last thing I needed was a staff member asking questions or, worse, chasing us off before I could see if I could pick up any relevant memories with my psychic nose. Or as Gilly liked to call it, my scratch-n-sniff visions.

So far, since we'd arrived on the cruise, my visions had been scarce. Other than the one intense flash in the elevator, all I'd caught were faint glimpses — hazy, sentimental memories. My guess? Most people on board were first-time cruisers, still too new to form deep emotional ties to the smells and spaces around them.

On the one hand, it was great news. I'd been working hard on blocking the more mundane emotional memories that gave me glimpses into people's personal lives. After the letter to the editor in the Garden Cove Gazette last year, calling me out as a psychic and accusing me of invading the privacy and personal thoughts of unsuspecting citizens, well, let's just say I'd worked even harder to control what I saw and when I saw it.

I was going to have to let some of that tightly held control loose now, though, if I wanted any hint as to what went down with Sebastian, leading up to his death.

"Anything?" Gilly asked.

"I haven't tried yet," I told her.

"All right," she said casually. "I'll be over here distracting any lookie-loos who might be curious."

"Much appreciated," I told her.

I squatted near the pool, still amazed at how well my knees were holding up since I'd started platelet-rich plasma injections with an orthopedic doctor four years ago. I'd been diagnosed with juvenile osteoarthritis in my teens, but I'd never let the pain in my joints hold me back. But when my later forties rolled around, the pain gradually worsened until I was in my fifties and struggling to go up and down stairs. When my doctor suggested the treatments, I was skeptical at first. Not anymore, though. The injections gave me so much pain relief and made my active lifestyle a heck of a lot more fun. The first two shots were six months apart, but since then, I'd only needed one shot a year.

"The hydrotherapy pool is closed," a middle-aged woman with bright bleach-blonde hair said with a snide tone. "You can't use it."

"We know," Gilly informed her in a "mind-yer-business" tone.

"Sorry," she said huffily. "But it doesn't seem like—"

"We can read a sign?" Gilly motioned with her hand dismissively. "No worries. We've made it through seventh grade." Then a bit like caveman speak, she added, "We know words good."

I coughed to cover the "hah!" that escaped my throat as the woman's eyes widened and she scurried off to lick her wounds. "You're on a roll, babe."

"We're on a mission to get this vacation back on

track, and nobody better try to stop us." She tapped her wrist. "Time's a wasting. Get to doing your thing."

"You're getting so bossy in your old age."

Gilly gasped. "Nora Black, you're not too big for me to whoop."

"That's probably true." I didn't try to stop the laugh this time. "Quit distracting me or we'll be here all day."

"Your daiquiri," I heard Bruno say.

"You're a doll," Gilly told him.

"What is your friend doing?" he asked.

"She's just sniffing the water."

I shook my head but tried to ignore her and concentrate on the scents of the hydrotherapy pool.

"Is that an American thing?" he asked.

"I don't think so," she said. "It's mostly just a Nora thing."

I turned my head over my shoulder to gawk at Gilly so fast I nearly gave myself whiplash. Bruno was standing next to her, and they were both watching me like I was a wild animal at the zoo.

Gilly took a long sip from a straw poking out of her bright red frozen drink. After she made a rolling gesture with her hand in my direction and told him, "It's better to observe from a distance and avoid interference." My bestie was in rare form.

"I see," the young man said, playing along. "I shall be guided by your experience in this matter."

I rolled my eyes before turning my attention back to the water. I noted a light, fresh odor coming from the pool, and only the barest hint of chlorine. Since Bruno looked like he was sticking around, I asked, "What do they use to treat the pool?"

"It has an ozone filtration system," he answered. "Top of the line. First class, all the way."

The clean scent was pleasant enough, but it wasn't inducing any helpful visions. What would the perpetrator have smelled? I concentrated on taking in the retreat's signature fragrance and the clean scent of ozone. The air the night before had been particularly briny, like fresh oysters on a half-shell. It wasn't as pronounced this morning, but the heat of the sun probably played a part in that.

I reached down and dragged my fingers across the water, breaking the surface tension, and without warning, a strong, vivid memory took hold.

*Inside an elevator, a figure is hunched and shadowed beneath an oversized hood of a large, shapeless rain jacket, dark orange like the ones they showed during the evacuation drill. With gloved hands, they press the button for the sixteenth floor. I can't tell if it's a man or a woman. The jacket's size and shape masks any sign of the person beneath it. Sebastian's limp body is slumped on the floor against the back wall. His face is blurred, but I recognize the wine stain on his white shirt.*

*The doors open, and the figure bends over, breath coming in harsh, uneven puffs. He or she grabs Sebastian's feet and drags him from the elevator car. His body is dead weight, awkward and unwieldy.*

*The figure glances around, then spots a nearby lounge*

*chair. With some effort, they heave Sebastian's body onto it, his arms dangling limply off the sides.*

*There are wheels on the back, but the lounger isn't made for hauling heavy objects, and the metal stabilizers near the middle drag against the deck until the figure lifts the front higher.*

*"Dammit," the person mutters, low, rough, making it annoyingly impossible to tell if it belongs to a man or a woman. The sound isn't grief or panic. It's frustration, sharpened by something darker.*

*The chair moves awkwardly but silently the rest of the way as they pull Sebastian to the hydrotherapy pool.*

*I grimace as Sebastian's head rolls lifelessly back and forth, confirming my suspicions that he is dead before he hits the water. It makes me sick to my stomach.*

*"You couldn't have waited until we were here to die?" the killer hisses, voice barely above a whisper. The words drip with venom. "A bastard until the very end."*

*They reach the hydrotherapy pool, the water calm and glassy, steam rising gently into the air. The scent of eucalyptus and lavender lingers...light, soothing, horribly relaxing and out of place for such a grim task.*

*The person rolls Sebastian out of the lounge near the edge of the water and then shoves his feet into the pool.*

*The first splash.*

*Next, they pushed the rest of the body in.*

*The second splash.*

*Spray from the splash causes the figure to step back, legs hitting the edge of the chair.*

*The second longer scraping sound.*

*Without a second look back, the person quickly makes their way back toward the elevator.*

"Oh, gosh," I gulp as the late morning sun's bright light welcomed me back to the present. I rocked forward unsteadily as I tried to stand up. Big mistake, as Julia Roberts said in Pretty Woman. Huge. I hadn't planned on swimming, but life didn't always go as expected. The next thing I knew, I'd gone headfirst into the proverbial dead body soup. I let out a yelp when I got my head above water and grabbed the side to keep from going under again.

"Nora!" Gilly exclaimed, no longer a casual observer.

"A little help, please," I said as she raced over to me.

Bruno had taken her daiquiri. His brow raised as he watched us struggle for a moment. Luckily, getting out of the water took only a few seconds.

"Towels, please," Gilly snapped at Bruno.

The young man put her drink down and hastily retreated toward the towel shack.

"Are you okay?" Gilly asked, smoothing my drenched hair away from my eyes. "That must have been a real doozy."

"It was." I nodded. "I saw the killer dump Sebastian's body. I was right, Gilly. He was dead long before he hit the water."

She frowned. "Well, poop."

"You were hoping I was wrong."

"It would've saved us a whole lot of time." She smiled as she patted my cheek. "Oh, well, nothing like murder to spice up a vacation."

The woman who'd told us the pool was closed, took the opportunity to walk past us and make a snide remark. "I guess seventh-grade educations aren't what they used to be."

Gilly's lip curled into a snarl.

I shook my head at my friend. "Let it go, babe. She's not worth it."

"Perhaps what this vacation needs are two murders."

Even though I knew she was joking, I said, "One is plenty, thank you very much."

"One what?" someone asked.

I shielded my eyes with my hand and looked up, immediately recognizing the slender-built and decidedly grumpy security chief.

"Chief Hansen," I greeted. "Fancy meeting you here. Again."

"What are you up to, Ms. Black?" she asked.

"Just relaxing with a dip in the pool."

"It's closed," she said.

"Oh, I know," I told her. "Just like I know that what happened here last night was no accident, and if that's the conclusion you decide to come to, I promise to raise a racket to anyone who will listen."

"What makes you think it's more than an accident?"

Other than the fact that the scraping sound I told her about last night couldn't have been made by Sebastian, which meant someone else had been there when he went into the water? I shook my head. "Call it gut, instinct, the fact that I'm not a gullible dimwit. I doubt very seriously your doctor is going to find any water in Sebastian's lungs. How can you have an accidental drowning if there is no one actually drowned."

"I told you to leave the investigating to me," she said, careful not to raise her voice.

"If you were investigating, then I would, but it seems to me you're trying really hard to sweep everything under the rug." I had no concrete proof she was trying to cover up a potential crime, except for my gut. The fact that she kept trying to get me to say the sounds I heard had happened in a different order the night before had only added to my suspicion that this was going to be deemed an accident, no matter the findings.

"That's it," Hansen said. "Do you want to be disembarked in Cozumel with the body? I can make that arrangement."

Gilly put her hand on my shoulder. "We don't want that."

"Good," the security chief said. "Now, stay out of it. I don't want to hear any more about you poking around in things that are not your concern." She gave me an "or else" glare before storming off.

Bruno brought four big fluffy towels over to us. "Everything okay here?" he asked.

"Fine," I groused as I took one and patted my wet hair. "Just great." I had a question about something I didn't understand in my vision that Bruno might be able to help with. "Is there an elevator back behind the bar area?"

"It's a service elevator," Bruno said. "It's for staff only."

"So, it doesn't go up to a penthouse suite or anything like that?"

"No," Bruno confirmed. "It only goes down to staff quarters, the galley, housekeeping, maintenance. You know. Services."

"Could a guest use the elevator?"

He gave me an odd but curious look. "They aren't supposed to, but I won't say it never happens."

"Interesting..."

He frowned. "Is it?"

"Very." I gave him a nod. "You've been a big help, Bruno. Thanks so much."

"My very pleasure." He gave us a playful bow, then went back to the bar to collect his next order.

When he out of earshot, Gilly gave me a wary look. "We're not staying out of it, are we?"

"Nope," I told her. "Not by a long shot. But I will be more careful going forward. The last thing I want is to get myself kicked off the ship."

"We'd sure miss you," Gilly said without missing a beat. She held her hand out and when I took it, she helped me to my feet. "Come on. Pippa will be waiting for us, and you'll need a change of clothes first."

"You know I love you, right?"

"I do. And I love you, too." She smiled. "But, Nora, if they boot you from the cruise, I'll be mad for you on your behalf, but I'm staying."

"That's fair," I told her as I put my arm around her shoulders, pressed my wet self against her side, and grinned as she made a face. "Totally fair."

I meant what I said about being more careful. I believed Hansen when she said I'd be disembarked, and I didn't want to leave the cruise any less than Gilly. Even so, I couldn't just ignore the fact that a man was murdered, even if the man was a big, dumb jerk who probably deserved what he got.

"Tacos," Gilly said to get me out of my head.

I forced a smile and nodded. "Tacos."

CHAPTER
# NINE

My wet pants stuck to my inner thighs with every step. By the time I reached the suite, I couldn't get them off fast enough. I happily peeled them away, along with the rest of my damp clothes, leaving them in a soggy heap on the floor. Gilly headed to her room to freshen up and use the bathroom while I hopped into the shower. Logically, I knew the ship's filtration system was top-notch, but Gilly calling the hydrotherapy pool "dead body soup" had planted itself firmly in my brain. I scrubbed harder than necessary, just to be sure.

Ten minutes later, I was clean, dressed, and mostly dry. I threw my wet clothes into the floor of the shower. Tinted sunscreen and a touch of blush gave me enough color to look alive, and I twisted my hair into a messy bun. Since Gilly wasn't knocking on my door, I wandered onto the balcony, letting the ocean breeze cool my skin. The rhythmic splash of waves lapping away from the ship was oddly calming. A small flock of seagulls circled below, one diving and resurfacing with a wriggling fish in its beak. Huzzah.

My eyes drifted to Callie's balcony. Had she come back to her room yet? It felt wrong not to check on her. It was the neighborly thing to do, and my mother hadn't raised me to be unneighborly.

The partition between our balconies was barely three feet tall, a slim sheet of aluminum more for territory division than privacy or security. It wasn't exactly Fort Knox. I swung a leg over, straddling it awkwardly before swinging my other leg over.

Easy peasy.

The curtains behind her sliding glass door were drawn open, and a bedside lamp cast a warm glow inside. Clothes were scattered haphazardly across the floor and strewn over the bed and couch. I knocked on the glass.

No answer.

I told myself to turn around. I'd checked. She wasn't there. My job was done. But my hand was already on the handle.

It wasn't locked.

That had to be a sign, right? If I wasn't supposed to go inside, the door would've been locked. A voice in my head called me out for the blatant nonsense, but it didn't matter. I couldn't shake the feeling something was wrong. What if Callie had slipped and hit her head in the shower? What if she was hurt? Or what if she wasn't the culprit, and whoever killed Sebastian, had injured Callie as well.

RENEE GEORGE

It wasn't a great excuse, but it was good enough for me.

I slid the door open and stepped inside. "Callie?" I said quietly. "Are you in here? Are you hurt? Do you need help?"

Silence answered.

The emerald-green dress Callie had worn to dinner was crumpled on the floor near the bed, a pair of heels overturned near the closet. Sebastian's wine-stained shirt was still on him when Ezra pulled his body from the pool, which told me he probably never returned to the room after dinner. But Callie's dress on the floor, said she had. So where had he gone after dinner? He mentioned meeting producers to pitch his show idea. Would he have gone without changing into something clean? Maybe. He hadn't seemed embarrassed by his streaky, uneven spray tan. Why would he care about a stain on his shirt?

The bathroom door stood wide open. The counter was littered with an explosion of makeup, cleansers, lotions, and beauty products. A curling iron was balanced upright in a bagless wastebin. Not a bad way to avoid burning yourself, I supposed. I went back out into the main part of the suite and began actively hunting for scented items. Maybe I could catch a memory that would reveal all.

"Nora Black!" Gilly hissed from the open balcony door. "What in the world are you doing?"

"Looking around," I said, like it was the most obvious thing in the world.

"Your investigation might not get you kicked off the

ship, but breaking and entering definitely will. Get out of there before someone catches you."

"Entering," I corrected her.

"What?"

"You said breaking and entering. The door wasn't locked, so I didn't break anything. I just entered."

"Semantics, really?" Gilly's expression was half-exasperation, half-amusement. "You're better than that."

I shrugged. "Am I, though?"

She pursed her lips, trying and failing to hide a smile. "This isn't funny."

I spread my hands in front of me, palms up. "I agree."

"Stop it," she said, but her voice wavered with suppressed giggles.

I gave her a pointed look. "Come in and help, or go back to your room."

"You're not the boss of me," she huffed, craning her neck to peek inside. "What exactly would I be helping with?"

"Look for anything that has a strong odor I can focus on."

She arched her brow at me. "Like dirty boxer shorts?"

I made a face and stuck out my tongue. "Gross. No. Whatever vision I'd get from that, I don't want it. Like, ever." I swiped the air in front of me as if I could erase the thought.

Gilly laughed. "Just trying to meet your investigative needs."

"If you really want to help, find a letter of confession.

That seems like the fastest way to wrap this whole thing up."

"Okey-dokey." She sighed as she reluctantly stepped inside. "One confession letter coming right up."

"Wouldn't it be nice if it was that easy?"

She looked at the alarm clock on the side table. "Our hour's nearly up. We'll have to go if we don't find anything in the next few minutes."

"Gotcha," I told her. Since we didn't have cell service, there was no way to let Pippa know if we were going to be late. "We'll leave in five minutes, vision or no vision."

"Unless we're in cruise jail," Gilly said. "You know, for *entering*."

I sniffed lotions, perfume bottles, cologne, hair spray, shampoo, conditioner...You name it. If it had a scent, I inhaled it. I wasn't getting anything.

"It's almost like she had no sentimental or emotional attachment to anything she owned." I scratched the base of my bun. "How's that even possible?"

"I have no idea," Gilly said. "I have an emotional attachment to my retired diaphragm."

"Well, yeah." I shot her a playful wink. "Bouncing Betty was always faithful, unlike all your exes."

"I *will* cut you," she threatened, a glint of humor in her eyes. She was searching through a Chanel carry-on bag and having as much luck as me. She glanced at the clock. "It's time to get going."

"I know." My shoulders dropped. My defeat complete. I wished invading Callie's privacy had borne any fruit. I would've taken a grape at this point.

"Hold up." Her hands were still inside the bag. "There's something behind the lining."

"Seriously?" I crossed the suite to her. "Can you get it?"

"Someone removed the lining and then reapplied it using Velcro." There was the tell-tale rip of one side of Velcro detaching from the other. Gilly slid her hand behind the lining and retrieved a plastic bag.

"What's in it?" I asked.

"It looks like letters, a small bottle of Vertiliance cologne, and a square of gray fabric." She unzipped the package and reached inside. "It feels like sweatshirt material, soft on one side and tight-knit on the other."

"That's an inexpensive cologne." I picked up the bottle. "I've seen it at Penny's for under thirty dollars." I opened the cap and took a good whiff.

*"God, I love the way you smell," a woman coos to her lover. They lay in bed, their arms and legs entwined. "I love the way you hold me." She slides his gray Indiana University sweatshirt up his body and over his head. "I love the heat of your body against mine, and the way you love me like no one else has ever loved me." I can't see their faces, of course, but I recognize Callie's voice. She trails a finger across his bare chest. This man has the body of someone young and in shape. The dancer Ramone? Doubtful. The man's hair is light brown.*

*"I'm gonna spend the rest of my life with you Callie Lee," he tells her. "There ain't no one else in this world for me but you. You are my entire world."*

*"And you're my universe, Billy Grant."*
*Billy? That was her first husband.*

*"Promise me," he says. "Promise me that it's you and me to the end."*

*"I promise," she replies. "I swear it to God. And after I get my record deal and make it big, I'm going to give you a dozen babies, and you can stay home and raise them while I bring home the bacon."*

*"Oh," he growls. "Now, I like that scenario. There ain't nothin' wrong with being a kept man."*

*She giggles as he rolls her onto her back and crawls on top. "As long as you get to keep me right back."*

I blinked as the world came back into focus, my gut churning with heartbreak and pain. She'd loved him. More than I could've imagined. Billy Grant hadn't been a steppingstone to bigger and better things for Callie. He'd been her one true love. Her everything. The fact that she had kept his cologne and what looked to be a square of the sweatshirt he'd been wearing in the vision, seemed to confirm it.

"Nora, you're crying." Gilly's voice sounded worried. "Are you okay?"

I shook my head but said, "I'm okay."

"All these letters are love notes written from Billy to Callie." She held up one of the unfolded letters. "What does this mean?"

My chest tightened as I started reassessing everything I'd thought about Callie, all my preconceived notions. "I think it means she's not the black widow I thought she was."

"So, you don't think she killed her first husband?"

I shook my head. "No. I don't think she did. These

96

things in this plastic bag are the only things she cares about out of all her possessions. I don't think she would have given him up for any reason. Not even winning a show."

"What about Sebastian? Do you think she killed him?"

That I was less confident about. Maybe she blamed him for what happened to Billy, and she'd been biding her time until she could take her revenge. Frankly, the idea seemed convoluted and unrealistic.

I met Gilly's gaze. "That remains to be seen." I gestured to the carry-on. "Put the letters and stuff back how you found them and let's go see Pippa and see what she could find out."

Maybe her research could offer insight that the visions weren't giving. One thing was for sure. In one fell swoop, she'd become someone I pitied. Because of that, I hoped she was innocent. Only time would tell.

## CHAPTER
# TEN

Pippa was waiting for us at High Seas Taqueria, nestled among five or six other small eateries, including Margherita Del Mar, a cozy pizzeria, The Stop, a carving station for the hungriest of carnivores, and a burger joint cleverly named The Burger Joint. The whole area buzzed with the scent of sizzling meat and warm tortillas, making my stomach growl in protest.

"What took you guys so long?" Pippa complained, crossing her arms. "I've been sitting here for half an hour." She raised her brows at us accusingly. "I almost left."

"I guess it's a good thing for us you didn't," I teased, flashing her a grin.

She scowled at me, but honestly, it was more adorable than intimidating.

"I sincerely apologize," I said, holding a hand over my heart for extra flair. "But I think you'll want to hear what I discovered."

"We," Gilly cut in with an exaggerated cough. "*We* discovered."

I nodded, pointing to her. "What she said."

Pippa leaned back in her chair, unimpressed. "I found out some stuff myself," she said, voice low and cryptic. "But first, let's get food. Breakfast is wearing thin, and I'm starving."

"And this is why we're friends." I didn't need more convincing. In seconds, we were all in line, eyes locked on the taco menu like it held the meaning of life.

"Oh, look," Pippa exclaimed, pointing past the line. "The table two down from ours."

I followed her gaze and spotted Carl and Augusta, the sweet retired couple from dinner, waving enthusiastically.

"Aww. It's Carl and Augusta!" I pressed my hands together over my chest in a heart shape. "I love them so much."

"Me too," Pippa agreed with a dreamy sigh. "They're the best."

Gilly's expression soured, her brows pinching together. "Who are they?"

"They're our tablemates in the main dining room," Pippa explained. "We met them last night."

Gilly's face fell, like she'd missed out on something special.

"Augusta is a retired civil lawyer, and her husband Carl is a retired top-rate pediatric gastroenterology surgeon." I paused for a moment to make sure I said it correctly. I was pretty sure I had. "I meant to ask Scott if he'd heard of him. Augusta says that surgeons world-wide still call him to consult about their cases."

"Wow," she said. "I really miss a lot. Scott would've loved to have met him."

"No worries, Pal." I gave her a friendly pat on the shoulder. "We'll introduce you after we order," I promised. "And Scott will get a chance to meet them at dinner one of these nights."

She perked right back up.

"Maybe we'll run into Helena and Jasper, the honey-mooners," Pippa said.

"They're from Kentucky," I told Gilly.

Pippa tilted her head, her expression skeptical.

"Did I mix them up in my head?" I asked, feeling a little unsure. "Was it Augusta and Carl from Kentucky? The guys started talking sports, and I filled the conversation in the words-in-words-out file in my brain."

"It's not that," she said slowly. "The way Jasper said Louisville makes me think he's not actually from there."

"How did he say it?"

"He called it Lou-ee-ville."

Gilly frowned. "That's... not how you say it?"

Pippa let out a soft snort of amusement. "I went there for training years ago. Almost got crucified by the locals for saying it that way. They insisted it's Lou-uh-vuhl, like your tongue's too lazy to finish the word." She shrugged. "I meant to mention it last night, but I forgot."

"They could be transplanted natives," I suggested, thinking aloud. "They've lived there long enough to call it home, but not long enough to pick up the accent."

"Possible," Pippa allowed. "But I was there one week and left sounding like a local."

Before I could respond, the man behind the counter cut in with a booming, cheerful voice. "*Buenos días*! Who wants tacos?"

I didn't hesitate. "I'll take one al pastor, one pork carnitas, and one birria."

"I'll do the same," Pippa added.

"Me too," Gilly said, making it an easy hat trick.

The man grinned. "Ah, *muy perfecto, mis amigas bonitas*! You're gonna love these. Best tacos on the whole ocean!"

"*Gracias*," Gilly thanked him, her grin matching his energy. "We're holding you to that."

He handed us a number, his grin widening as he looked at Gilly. "For you, *bonita*, I'll make them with extra love. If they're not the best tacos you've ever had, you come back and let me try again. Deal?"

"Deal," she replied. When we walked away, my best friend of over fifty years had a little kick in her step. "I still got it," she muttered. Gilly had the thickest, wavy brown hair—from a bottle these days, but let those of us without any gray coverage cast the first stone—big brown eyes and curves for days. At fifty-six, she still knew how to bring all the boys to the yard.

"Damn straight," I concurred. "Come on." I nodded toward Carl and Augusta's table. "Time for introductions."

We made our way over, dodging other passengers lining up for food.

"Hey, you guys," I greeted them with a wave. "Fancy meeting you here."

"Nora, Pippa," Augusta said warmly. "It's so nice to run into you. And this must be your seasick friend, Gilly."

"That would be me." Gilly plastered on her friendliest smile. "I'm only sorry we didn't get to meet last night. Nora said you're a lawyer, and Carl is a pediatric surgeon."

"Guilty as charged," Augusta sang jovially. "On all counts."

"Lawyer joke." Gilly snorted a laugh. "Very clever."

Carl chuckled softly. "She likes to think so."

Gilly added a dramatic flourish with her hands. "Well, if you can't dazzle them with brilliance..."

"...baffle them with bull," Augusta finished, grinning wide.

"Oh, I like you," Gilly said, laughing. "I'm keeping you."

Carl gazed at his wife with a mixture of love and pride. "She's a total catch."

"Oh, Carl." Augusta pished him, but a rosy flush in her cheeks gave away her pleasure. I couldn't believe they'd been married for forty years. If marriages were a competition, they would've taken the gold. "He's such a sweet-talking charmer," she said. "It's the reason I told him no the first time he asked me out for a date."

"And the second time, and the third," Carl tacked on playfully. "I finally had to have a friend of mine intervene on my behalf."

"I thought anyone as slick and as sure of himself as

Carl Frank would be nothing but trouble." She cast a sideways glance at him. "He's proved me right every day."

Now it was Carl's turn to pish. It was about that time that the couple seemed to realize they had company. "I'm so sorry," Augusta gushed. "We're monopolizing the whole conversation."

"I'm loving every minute of it," Gilly confided. "It gives me hope for the future."

"Me too," Pippa agreed. "Did you all have children?"

"No," Carl said quickly. "Not in this lifetime." He reached across the table and took her hand. "But she's all I've ever needed."

"You old dog." Augusta blushed again. She smiled at us. "You want to know the secret to forty years? Forty-three if you count the dating years."

"I'd love to know the secret," Gilly said. "I'm on husband number two, and I want him to be husband number last."

Personally, I didn't think she had anything to worry about. The way Carl looked at Augusta was the same way Scott looked at her.

Augusta leaned forward, drawing us in. "I wake up every morning and ask myself, am I happy? If the answer is yes, I keep doing what I'm doing. If the answer is no, then I figure out what I need to do to get back to happy, and I work it out."

"That simple, huh?" I asked.

Her wide smile lit up her eyes. "And that hard." She

laughed. "But having Carl by my side makes it a heck of a lot easier."

"*Och- ocho!*" the guy at the taqueria shouted out. "Eight-eight!"

"That's us!" Gilly held up the ticket. "So nice to meet you both. Hopefully we'll see each other at dinner."

"I'm sure we will," Augusta said as a farewell. "Enjoy your lunches."

We retrieved our tacos and scarfed them down like ravenous hyenas...

"These are so good." I was practically melting in my seat as the spice danced on my tongue. "I could eat here every day, and since the food is all-inclusive, I think I will."

"We're not going to eat tacos every day for lunch," Pippa stated.

I gave her a bland look. "Maybe you won't, but I'm good with eating lunch wherever you want. Then I'll have second lunch at the Taqueria."

She shook her head. "This world is your taco journey and the rest of us are just living in it."

"That is correct." I took the last bite of the birria taco, the spicy juice from the meat dripping down my chin as I finished chewing and swallowed it down. "I've been wanting to try a birria taco ever since I saw a social media chef make them. I wiped my chin with a napkin. "Totally worth the hype."

"They are super delish," Gilly agreed.

Pippa shook her head and frowned. "A little spicy for

my taste. If we do this again, I'm swapping out for the shredded chicken."

I called her out. "Weenie."

"Wimp," Gilly piled on.

"I have a delicate palate, you big bullies," she informed us.

In the distance, we could hear music starting up.

"The Lido Deck pool party must be starting up." The itinerary had a list of multiple events meant to keep guests happy and busy during the at-sea days. A familiar tune began to play.

Pippa let out a soft cry as Chappell Roan started singing Pink Pony Club.

"Aww, honey." I got up and moved my chair next to her. Gilly did the same on the other side. "It's okay."

"I didn't think I'd miss them this much." She dabbed at her eyes. "We've only been gone for a day and a half, but I can't help but wonder what new thing JayJay is learning, or what new skill J.P. will master while I'm gone."

I wanted to say, "It's only a week," but as the only non-mother of the group, I decided I probably wasn't the person to tell her to suck it up.

Thank heavens, Gilly knew how to handle it. "I remember the first time I left the twins. I felt the same way. I cried every night, and Gio and I even cut our weekend away short, because I couldn't stand being away from them." She rubbed Pippa's back. "But you know what, they were perfectly happy at home, and I'd traumatized myself for no good reason. It's more than okay that you're missing them, though. But you know Tippy is taking great care of them both."

I nodded. "Besides, it's not like we can ask the captain to turn the ship around."

"You're right. You're both right." Pippa blew her nose. "I called them from the WiFi bar last night," she admitted sheepishly. "I'll probably do it again tonight."

"And you absolutely should," Gilly encouraged. "Mommy blues are real, and sometimes you need to get your fix."

"Are you equating my kids to drugs?"

Gilly hummed an "mmmm," then said, "Nothing beats new baby smell."

"This is verging on disturbing," I told them, ending the comment with a laugh. "I suggest distraction. We have news. You have news. Let's share."

"Good idea." Pippa sniffled. "You first."

Since we were close together now, I kept my volume low as I told her about my vision at the hydrotherapy pool.

It was Pippa's turn to laugh, when Gilly declared, "And then she fell in the pool."

"Har har." I reached over Pippa's lap and flicked Gilly's thigh.

"Ouch," she said slowly for effect.

I ignored her. "In the room, Gilly found a secret stash of mementos from Callie's first husband."

"It was inside the lining of a Chanel bag," Gilly confirmed. "The lining had been modified with Velcro to hide a small bottle of cologne, a square of sweatshirt fleece, and a small stack of love letters."

"Seriously?" Pippa's eyes were wide.

"Seriously." I lowered my voice even more. "When I smelled the cologne, I got a really intimate memory of the two of them, Callie and Billie Grant. They were so much in love it hurt." I gave her a play-by-play of what I could remember. When I finished, I touched my chest. "And I mean, hurt."

"Nora cried," Gilly added nonchalantly.

I pivoted my gaze to her. "Do you want to get flicked again?"

"Nope." She scooted her chair out of my reach.

"That's so sad," Pippa said, her brow wrinkled in thought. "It kind of goes hand in hand with what I found out."

"And what was that?"

"Billy Grant, the adopted son of William and Leta Grant, had been estranged from his family for years. Apparently, he suffered from depression off and on throughout his childhood. His parents were of the suck-it-up-butter-cup school of child-rearing. He went to college at Indiana University where he met Callie and dropped out his junior year to work full-time to support her dream of becoming a singer after they got married."

None of this seemed revelatory. "The history of depression supports the idea that he committed suicide, right? So why did they initially list it as suspicious?"

Pippa nodded. "Yes. The forensics does as well. There

was nothing to indicate he was pushed from the window of his hotel room." She pursed her lips. "This information wasn't in the news or given to any journalists. Reese contacted a friend at the Los Angeles PD. When she asked them why they suspected foul play, her friend told her that they found an email chain between Callie and Billy, where Callie actively encouraged him to end his life."

Gilly gasped. I'm pretty sure I did as well. "No." I couldn't believe the woman I'd seen holding Billy in bed could ever do something so heinous. "Why would she do that?"

"After a thorough investigation by their cybercrime unit, it was determined that Callie, in fact, hadn't sent those emails. It was someone else."

"Who?" Gilly scooted forward. "Who did it?"

Pippa shrugged. "They could never trace where the IP originated, but Reese's friend said that there were rumors it was Sebastian Caldwell. They never had any evidence to support the rumors, though, so they finally closed the case, and put Billy Grant's death to bed."

"Holy cow." I pressed my chest again. It was getting uncomfortably tight. "Poor Billy. And poor Callie. I wonder if she knew about the rumors."

"Are you okay?" Gilly's face pinched with worry. "That's the third or fourth time I've seen you touch your chest today. Are you having pain?"

"Nothing bad," I told her. "I'm sure it's just stress. Maybe a little indigestion."

"You should get it checked out."

"I'm fine." I brushed off her suggestion. "What about

the recording of Callie telling Billy she'd kill him on the podcast you listen to."

"A total fabrication," Pippa stated, her face incredulous. She threw up her hands. "They used AI to fake the voices."

"God, I hate AI," I said. "It's the worst." My neck felt uncomfortably warm and tense. "Maybe I should go to the medical clinic."

Both my friends were out of their chairs.

"Don't make a fuss," I told them. "It's probably the birria tacos. They really were spicy."

"See," Pippa said. "Not a wimp or a weenie."

They linked their arms in mine, and together, our dynamic trio headed to the nearest elevator.

CHAPTER

# ELEVEN

octor Patel, who had been called to the Resplendent Retreat the night before to examine Sebastian's body and declare the time of death, was on duty. His eyebrows lifted slightly when he saw me walk through the clinic doors, flanked by Gilly and Pippa.

"Mrs. Black, isn't it?" he asked, watching as my friends guided me to a chair.

I didn't bother to correct him, Ms., not Mrs., because frankly, I was too uncomfortable to care.

"We think she might be having a heart attack," Gilly blurted, her voice edged with panic.

"I'm not having a heart attack," I insisted, though their concern had started to wear on me, making the ache in my chest and neck tighten even more.

"When did it start?" the doctor asked as he pulled a stethoscope from a drawer.

"I'm not sure," I admitted. "I've felt a little off all day. There's been some pressure, but I figured it was stress."

"Understandable," he said with a nod. "I'm sure last night was difficult for you."

He placed the stethoscope's cold metal end to my chest and listened, humming thoughtfully as he moved it around. Once he was done, he grabbed an electric blood pressure cuff connected to a monitor, along with a pulse oximeter.

I felt like an idiot. "It's probably just indigestion. I've been indulging in a lot of rich food since we boarded."

"That's possible," Dr. Patel acknowledged, "but better safe than sorry. I'll do an EKG, as well. Lower the collar of your shirt for me."

I tugged down the scoop neck on my shirt, and he attached a cardiac pad, a sticky white circle with a metal nipple on the left side of my upper chest.

"Raise your shirt on the left side," he directed. When I did, he stuck another pad on my ribs to the side of my heart. After, he took some wires from below the monitor and attached them to the pads. "There," he said. "All done."

While the cuff inflated, squeezing my arm uncomfortably, I decided to ask the question burning in my mind. "So, Doc, did you find out what really happened to Sebastian? It wasn't drowning, right?"

His eyes narrowed slightly. "No. Not drowning. There was no water in his lungs. If it gives you any peace of mind, you and your husband couldn't have saved him, no matter how quickly you got him out of the pool or how long you performed CPR."

"Husband," Gilly snickered under her breath.

"Ezra's not my husband," I clarified, but didn't bother explaining. "If it wasn't drowning, do you think it could've been foul play?"

The cuff tightened to an almost unbearable degree, making me wince.

"Not at all," the doctor said firmly. "If you must know, the evidence suggests he likely had a stroke. His platelet count and clotting factors were elevated. It looks like he most likely threw a clot and fell into the pool when he died."

My stomach twisted. That didn't align with what I heard and saw in my vision. Someone had pushed Sebastian into the pool. But if he was already dead, maybe they hadn't killed him. So why make it look like a drowning?

The cuff hissed as it deflated, releasing my arm with a sharp ache. I glanced at the monitor. My oxygen level was ninety-two percent, and my pulse was ninety-two...way higher than normal for me.

"Could he have ingested something that caused the elevated platelet count?" I asked, grasping at straws.

Dr. Patel gave me a long, disapproving look. "Why are you so determined to make this more than it is?"

"Because there was someone else on the deck with Sebastian," I said, my voice rising. "Ezra and I heard them." I threw up my arm in frustration, forgetting about the leads stuck to my chest. They tugged uncomfortably at my skin. "Why is everyone so determined to call it an accident or natural causes?"

"I follow the science, Mrs. Black. No more, no less."

He glanced back at the machine, studying the results. "Your blood pressure is elevated, but not dangerously high. Your pulse is fast, but your EKG shows a normal sinus rhythm at this time."

"And that means...?" I prompted. My mind flashed to the last time I'd died — twenty-seven seconds of no heartbeat, no breathing, and a vivid trip to the afterlife. When they brought me back, I came back different, with a psychic gift. A blessing and a curse, depending on the day. I didn't want to experience death again to see what else I might wake up with.

"With your elevated heart rate, blood pressure, and slightly low oxygen levels," he explained, "I think you're experiencing angina, a temporary reduction of blood flow to the heart."

He unlocked a cabinet, took out a small bottle of pills, and handed one to me. "This is sublingual nitroglycerin. Put it under your tongue. If the pain eases quickly, it's a good indication that my diagnosis is correct."

I popped the pill under my tongue. "Now-ah wahaat?" I mumbled, trying to talk around it.

"We wait."

Gilly and Pippa hovered nearby, their faces drawn tight with worry. The fact that neither of them was talking only made me more anxious. But within minutes, the pressure in my chest started to ease. My breathing came easier, and the tension in my neck faded.

I frowned at Dr. Patel. "It worked."

"That's good news, Mrs. Black."

"No, it means I have angina."

"And it's manageable," he said calmly. "I'll prescribe you some nitroglycerin to keep on hand during the cruise, and I want you to start taking a daily aspirin. It'll help prevent another attack."

I nodded numbly, trying to process it all. Angina wasn't a death sentence, but it sure wasn't something I wanted to add to my already complicated life.

"What about the cruise this week? Is there anything I should or shouldn't do?" I asked him.

If he said *leave the investigating to the investigators*, I was going to punch him.

"You should be fine," he said instead. "Relax when you can, and if you can't, stay vigilant about any signs of another attack. If you feel chest pain or pressure, take a nitroglycerin pill immediately. If you're having pain before starting an activity, don't do it. And when you get home after the cruise, make sure to follow up with a cardiologist."

Fantastic. Getting older was so much fun. *Not.*

Still, it was better than the alternative.

"Also, I'd like you to come back for a check-up in a few days so I can recheck your blood pressure and see how you're feeling."

"I was really hoping this was just indigestion," I muttered.

"Well, it's not," Gilly said, finally speaking again. "We'll make sure she's here for that check-up, Doc."

"Avoid alcohol and smoking," he said. "They can aggravate the condition."

"Well, I'd hate to aggravate the angina," I said a bit sarcastically. "That might piss it off." I knew I was acting like a brat, so I course-corrected myself. "I'm sorry, Doctor Patel. I appreciate your advice and your help. I feel much better because of your expertise, and I won't take that for granted."

He looked mildly surprised at my apology, then genuinely pleased. "Thank you, Mrs. Black. People come to me sick and worried, and that can cause them to act like regular—"

"Jerks," I supplied.

"Yes, exactly so." He smiled. "I appreciate your self-awareness and your apology, but please note that I don't take it personally."

"It's Ms. Black," I told him. "I'm not married. You can call me Nora, though, if it's easier."

His smile widened. "Thank you, Nora." He picked up an electronic tablet from the counter. "I'm sending your order for sublingual nitroglycerin to take as needed for angina pain to the pharmacy, and you'll have to get the aspirin off the shelf. It's an over-the-counter medication."

After the doctor discharged me and we left the clinic, Pippa sighed. "Well, that's something new to worry about."

"I won't worry if you don't," I said, trying to sound lighthearted.

"As if," she huffed. "When we get you back home, we're—"

"I'll talk to a doctor and follow whatever they recommend," I cut in before she could start listing all the ways she planned to smother me with love and concern.

When we reached our corridor, I wrapped my arms around both of them, pulling us into a tight hug. There may or may not have been a few tears, but what happens in the pity circle stays in the pity circle.

"I don't know what I'd do without you guys," I said when the elevator dinged open and we finally broke apart.

"You'll never have to find out," Gilly promised.

"Because I'm going to die before you?" I teased, trying to break the tension.

"Too soon!" Pippa scolded, shaking her head. "Way too soon for jokes."

I chuckled softly. "Noted."

It was getting late, and Ezra and the guys were probably finishing up their golf game. They'd be heading back to the suites soon. What was I supposed to say to him? How did I explain that I'd basically had a warning shot for a heart attack? If Pippa and Gilly hadn't bullied me into going to the clinic, it could've turned into something way worse. I hated to think about it, but I was so grateful for them. I might've been an only child, but they made me a sister. Family wasn't just blood — and since all my blood relatives, aside from a few distant cousins, were gone, they were my family now. Gilly, Pippa, their kids, their husbands, Ezra, and even Mason. My chosen family. I couldn't believe how lucky I was that they chose me back.

We stepped off the elevator onto our floor. Housekeeping was still moving between rooms, pushing their carts and swapping out towels. Hopefully, they'd already been to ours. I didn't need much, just fresh towels and more coffee.

Halfway down the corridor, a man stepped out of a maintenance closet. He carried a medium-sized plastic tub with a picture of a rat on the front, covered by a red circle and a line slashed through it.

Holy smokes. The ship had a rat problem.

"Huh," I grunted. My conspiracy theory about Hansen hiding the security footage to cover up what really happened might've been wrong after all. If the ship did have rats, and ugh, I didn't even want to picture that. Maybe they had chewed through the camera wires. Gross, but plausible. "Well, crap."

"What?" Pippa asked, her voice sharp with concern. "Are you okay? You're not having pain again, are you?"

"No," I assured her. "I'm fine. But I think I owe Chief Hansen an apology."

"Wow." Gilly's mouth quirked into a half-smile. "An apology tour. First the doctor, now the security chief. Who's next?"

"It won't be you," I shot back playfully.

As we reached our suite, I heard muffled laughter and voices from inside. These walls were definitely not soundproof. I wasn't ready to tell Ezra about the angina yet. He'd fuss over me, and the last thing I wanted was for him to start seeing me as fragile or sick.

Still, it was time to face the music.

I gestured toward Gilly and Pippa as they opened their doors. "See you on the other side."

When Gilly's face fell, I added quickly, "Of the room. You know, the balcony."

"I know," she said, sounding defensive, but her smile returned.

With that, we all headed inside to join our men.

# TWELVE

The ocean stretched endlessly beyond the railing as distant laughter from other decks floated on the air.

We lounged on the balcony furniture, listening as the guys recounted their indoor golf adventures. Ezra bogeyed, Scott nailed a hole-in-one, and Jordy somehow managed an eagle. They'd played as a team against another group and ended with a combined score of 83...mostly thanks to Scott, who, apparently, was a golf prodigy, according to Ezra and Jordy.

What did that all mean? It meant they'd had a blast, and I was about to kill the vibe with my news.

I needed to tell Ezra first. Dropping my health scare on him in front of everyone wasn't fair. I shifted closer to him and touched his arm. "Hey, I need to talk to you for a moment. Alone, if that's okay?"

"Of course." His brow furrowed as he studied my face. "Did I do something?"

I let out a soft laugh. "No, you didn't do anything. I just need to tell you about something that happened today."

"Something that happened to you?" His voice sharpened with concern. His eyes searched mine. "Let's go inside." He glanced over at Scott and Jordy. "Be back in a bit."

They gave noncommittal grunts of acknowledgment, already diving back into their golf recap with Pippa and Gilly.

Inside the suite, the room was cool and dim compared to the balcony. Housekeeping had come earlier, and the bed was made, fresh towels hung neatly in the bathroom, and the faint scent of lavender from the housekeeping spray still lingered.

Ezra rested his hands gently on my shoulders, his thumbs brushing over the tops of my arms. He leaned down, eyes level with mine. "What happened?"

I swallowed hard. "I don't want you to get upset..."

"Like a Band-Aid, Nora. Rip it off. It'll hurt less in the long run."

We were about to find out. I took a breath. "I had a minor, teensy-weensy angina attack this afternoon."

His face went from surprised to worried, then confused, then back to worried...a full circle of emotions in less than three seconds. "When? How?"

"At lunch," I admitted, fiddling with the hem of my shirt. "Apparently, a lot of things can cause it. Gilly and Pippa dragged me to the clinic, and Doctor Patel figured it out."

Ezra's brows knitting together. "Did he give you nitroglycerin?"

I blinked, startled. "How did you know that?"

His voice stayed low and steady, a calm undercurrent to my churning nerves. "I know things, Nora. Did it help?"

"Really fast," I said, my fingers tracing the seam of his shirt now. "I'm supposed to pick up a prescription at the pharmacy."

"Then we should go do that." He didn't hesitate. Instead, he treated it like any other errand on a to-do list, not a follow-up to a heart scare.

I wasn't sure what I'd expected, maybe panic or an over-the-top reaction. Ezra wasn't built for that, though. "Easy" wasn't just his nickname. He'd been weathered by life young. A dad at sixteen, a husband before he graduated high school, working full-time, then putting himself through college to become a detective. He wasn't a man who buckled. He absorbed life's punches and kept moving. I didn't want to be another beating he had to take on.

"*We* don't have to do anything," I said quickly, the words tumbling out. "I don't want to be a problem for you to fix." I slid my arms around his waist, pressing my cheek to his chest, where his heartbeat thumped slow and sure. "You don't have to take care of me." I leaned back to meet his gaze. "I'm really good at taking care of myself."

A flicker of anger tightened his jaw, but it passed as fast as it came. "Yes, you are, babe," he said gently, his hands moving to my back and rubbing slow circles. "You're great at taking care of yourself. But I love you, and it makes me happy when you let me in enough to help. I know it's hard for you to let someone else take a burden off your shoulders, and if it really makes you uncomfortable, I'll back off. But I want to be here for you like you're there for everyone else, including me. I want you to know that you can rely on me no matter what. I just want to love you the way you deserve to be loved, Nora. So, let me, okay?"

His words moved me, but they also made me afraid. "I'm not an invalid, you know. I am really good at bouncing back."

"I know that." He sighed, his hands resting on my hips. "Are you going to let me help you?"

A breathy chuckle escaped me. "I guess so. But only because you've got a cute butt."

He let out a surprised laugh, the tension cracked. He leaned in, brushing his lips over mine, the kiss slow and sweet until my knees wobbled like jelly.

"Can we go get your medicine now?" he murmured against my lips.

"Yes." I sighed, kissing him back, lingering just a second longer. "We probably should."

"I'll let the others know we'll be back soon."

"Good." I caught his hand before he could walk away, lacing my fingers through his. He glanced back, curious. I smiled up at him, warmth blooming in my chest. "Thank you."

"For what?" he asked, voice soft.

"For showing me every day what real love should feel like."

He kissed me. "Every day for as long as you'll have me."

---

GOING to the pharmacy after four o'clock in the afternoon was an actual nightmare. The pill dispensary was more like a closet than a store, and the line to pick up medications was out the door and down the corridor.

"Holy moly," I whispered. "How many prescriptions does Doctor Patel write in a day?"

"A lot, apparently." Ezra stood behind me, his body pressed against my back and his arms wrapped around the front of my waist. "I can wait in the line and hold your place if you want to sit down until the line shortens." My shoulders must've tensed because he tacked on, "But only if you want to and not because I think you're an invalid."

His tone was teasing, so I swiftly tapped him in the side with my elbow.

"Oof," he said dramatically, rubbing his side.

"That didn't hurt."

He shook his head. "You don't know your own strength."

"Har har." While we made the journey to the pharmacy, I'd quietly filled Ezra in on both the visions, what Pippa had learned from Reese, and what Dr. Patel had said about Sebastian dying from a stroke. He'd been suitably impressed with all the information we'd gathered while he and the boys had been playing golf.

"Oh, and the rat thing on the ship is a real problem, apparently. I saw a maintenance guy with a tub of poison earlier." I shivered at the thought. "Who knew?"

"You know there's a reason for the phrase, 'like rats off a sinking ship.' The old seafaring ships always had rats on them, and if the boat was sinking, the rats were always the first ones to go overboard."

"So, you're saying that if a rat takes a dive off a rail, I should follow it in?"

"Yep, that's exactly what I'm saying." He shook his head.

"Ezra! Nora!" a woman called out.

We both turned to see Helena Peabody, the young bride half of the honeymoon couple, heading in our direction.

When she got to us, she asked, "Have either of you seen Callie or Sebastian?"

I shook my head, debating on whether I should tell her that Sebastian was dead, and Callie was missing. "Why?"

"Callie was supposed to meet me for some hot yoga this morning and she didn't show."

Hot yoga sounded...well, it sounded hot. No, thank you. If I wanted to be hot, I would skip swapping my hormone patch out for a week. I'd have all the hot I could stand. "I wish I could help," I told her. I thought about what Pippa had said about Kentucky. "Did I hear Jasper right last night? You all are from Louisville." I made sure the hit the is with a long e sound. Helena didn't bat an eyelash.

"We sure are," she said, putting on a thick accent as if talking about Kentucky brought out the backwoods in her.

"Huh." I forced a smile. I'd thought the couple pleasant and likable the night before, but now I could see there was something not quite right about them. "Cool," I told her. "Go Cardinals."

"What?" Helena's expression clouded over for a moment, then she said, "Yes, of course. Go, Cardinals." Her voice was bubbly and cheerful. "Well, if you run into her today, will you let her know I'm looking for her."

"You got it." I gave her a thumbs up.

When she left, Ezra leaned to my ear. "A thumbs up? Really?"

He was asking fate for another elbow to the ribs. "What do you want from me? I'm struggling here."

"What's got your hackles up about Helena?" he asked.

"It was Pippa. She said the way they said Louisville was all wrong for someone from there. It's pronounced *Lew-uh-vuhl*." I tried to drop off on the end the way Pippa had. "She said that she spent a week there, and that her pronunciation of the city was challenged and corrected by locals every time she opened her mouth." I tugged my lower lip between my teeth then let it go. "It's one thing not to correct someone when they get a word wrong, but it's another altogether to be a native to the area and get it wrong."

"That makes sense. Nice pick up, Pip."

"You'll have to let her know. She's feeling a bit vulnerable right now because she's missing her kids. It'll make her feel good to get the compliment. She really came through today with the information she got from Reese and the whole Louisville thing."

"Lying about where you're from doesn't make you a murderer, though," Ezra cautioned.

"I agree with you," I countered. "However, it does make you a liar and probably means you have something to hide." I tapped my chin. "I wish I knew what though."

The line finally moved a few feet, then stopped again. "We'll be here all the way through dinner if they don't kick it into high gear. People will die of old age in line before their illnesses take them."

My gaze drifted out over the scads of travelers going in and out of shops. At one point, I saw a neatly curled head of blonde hair and smiled. It was Augusta. She was coming out of one of the many WiFi lounges on the ship. I didn't see Carl. I was somewhat surprised, but I supposed they weren't joined at the hip.

"Hey," I alerted Ezra. "Look, there's Augusta." I pointed in the direction of the older woman.

Someone unexpected appeared right behind her. It was Rebecca Hansen. Was it a coincidence? I thought so at first, but then Augusta stopped, turned to Hansen, and they spoke for a few seconds, before Augusta went the opposite direction of the pharmacy, and Hansen was walking in our general direction.

I leaned my head back on Ezra's chest. "She threatened to kick me off the ship earlier."

"She did?"

I guess I'd forgotten to tell him about that, too. "Yep. She said if I didn't stop poking my nose in the cruise's investigation, she'd arrange for me to disembark permanently in Cozumel."

"Dang," Ezra said. "That's harsh."

"Way harsh," I agreed. As Hansen got closer, she saw us. She halted, and I wondered if she was debating going the other way. She must have grown a pair because she started our way again.

"Ms. Black, Mr. Holden," she hailed. "It looks like we're destined to keep crossing paths."

"Ms. Hansen," I greeted back. "Looks like." I really wanted to ask her about Augusta and why they were talking, but I wanted to stay out of the brig and on the ship more. "Have you let Callie Caldwell know about her husband yet?" I asked in a hushed voice.

"Still looking," she replied.

"Also, I want to apologize," I said with real contrition. "I know there's a rat on the ship."

"There's a what?" she asked alarmed.

"Or rats." I put my hands down at my sides. "I saw a maintenance guy carrying some rat poison around." Every time I thought of the large rodents running around the ship my teeth hurt. "Anyhow, I accused you of sabotaging the camera, and I'm sorry."

Her brows knitted together. "You didn't accuse me of that."

I winced. "My inside voice did."

"It's fine." Hansen laughed. "My inside voice is always accusing someone of something, and sometimes it's just mean and nasty for no reason."

I grinned. "Probably not *no* reason."

"Not *not* no," she allowed. With the first genuine smile I'd seen from her, Hansen made her farewell. "It was almost pleasant, Ms. Black."

"Almost."

After she left, Ezra remarked, "If I didn't know better, I might think the two of you could be friends."

"But you do know better." The memory of her pushing us to change our statements stuck with me. It wasn't just incompetence. It felt deliberate like she'd wanted the truth buried. Suspicious deaths were bad for business, after all. Still, I couldn't shake the feeling there was more to it. And it was odd she hadn't been able to find Callie. Maybe the Ultimate Singer of America had decided to jump ship.

My mind drifted to Ramone...tall, dark, and handsome. I was ninety-eight percent sure, okay, maybe ninety-seven percent, he was the guy we'd seen Callie with in the perfume shop. He might be the key to tracking her down. Lucky for me, I knew exactly where to find him without drawing attention.

The line inched forward, and the crowd groaned, annoyed at gaining only two feet before halting again. I glanced back at Ezra. "You want to learn Latin ballroom dancing with me tonight?"

His brow lifted, amusement tugging at his mouth.

"What kind of partner would I be if I said no? Besides, it takes two to tango."

Perfect. Something told me Ramone was my best shot at finding Callie. She might look like a black widow, but my gut said she was more of a trapped fly. If I could help her, I would.

# THIRTEEN

inner was just the six of us. None of our other tablemates showed up, which was a letdown. I'd been hoping to see Augusta and Carl again, and my curiosity about Helena and Jasper was still nagging at me.

"We make port in Cozumel at eight tomorrow morning," Jordy said, eyeing me carefully. "Are you okay with everyone doing their excursions?"

"I am," I replied. They didn't need my permission, but ever since the angina scare, they'd all been tiptoeing around me like I might shatter. "Whatever happens is going to happen. If we can't figure out who pushed Sebastian in the pool by morning, I'm going to let it go."

Gilly choked on her water, coughing behind her napkin. "That'll be a first." She dabbed at her mouth. "You're a dog with a bone, sometimes. Just gnawing away even after it's past its expiration date."

"Not this time," I insisted, lifting my chin. "After

tonight, it's going to be chill-vibes Nora for the rest of the trip."

"I can't wait to meet chill-vibes Nora," Pippa teased. "I bet she's a hoot and a holler."

"Me too," Gilly piled on. "It sounds like we're getting a BFF upgrade."

"You two are pure comedy gold," I shot back at them. "Take that show on the road."

Our laughter lightened the mood, the earlier tension fading.

"So, Gilly tells me the doctor said Sebastian's platelets were high, and he might've had a stroke," Scott said, steering the conversation back to business.

"That's what Doctor Patel said." I met his gaze. "You're a doctor. Can you tell if someone had a stroke after death with just a blood test?"

"It's not that simple." Scott steepled his fingers, thinking. "A high platelet count suggests he was throwing clots, but without an autopsy, there's no certainty."

"And if the cause of death is listed as natural or accidental, there won't be an autopsy," Ezra added.

"Exactly." Scott shrugged. "It's a frustrating loophole. Autopsies are expensive, and insurance doesn't cover them. The police will if it's part of an investigation, but if it's ruled accidental? No dice."

"It's always about money," Gilly sighed.

"It usually is," I agreed. "It keeps the world spinning and stops it cold in its tracks just as fast."

I scanned the dining room for Charise. Instead, a

young Latino man approached the table, a polite but reserved expression on his face. He was lean, maybe in his early twenties, with neatly combed black hair and sharp brown eyes. His uniform was crisp, but his sleeves were a little too long, making him look like a kid playing dress-up.

"I'm Domingo," he said, his voice smooth and quiet. "I'll be your steward this week. Are we ready to order?"

"I thought Charise was our steward," Jordy said, frowning.

Domingo shifted his weight from foot to foot. "Charise has been transferred to another section of the dining room," he said, clearing his throat. "At her request."

"I can't say I blame her," Pippa said. "I wouldn't want to serve the man who publicly annihilated me and my career on live television in front of millions of people."

I winced. "When you put it like that..."

"Give us five minutes, Domingo," Ezra said, his tone friendly but firm. "We'll be ready to order."

Domingo nodded once, crisp and polite, then walked away.

"So, is Charise still a suspect?" Gilly asked.

I inclined my head in the affirmative. "Yes, but not a strong one."

Ezra leaned forward, his elbows on the table. "If she killed Sebastian, she'd probably have stayed on our service. She'd want to show she didn't hold a grudge. Moving sections makes me think she expected him to come back."

I pointed at Ezra with my thumb. "What he said."

"Most criminals aren't masterminds, though," Ezra continued. "And Charise does have a strong motive."

"Which is why she's still on the list," I conceded.

"Who else is on the list?" Scott asked.

"Callie, of course," I said. "The spouse is always a suspect. The not-from-Louisville couple, too. I don't know if they're hiding something connected to Caldwell's death, but they're definitely hiding something. Then there's Rebecca Hansen—"

"The security chief?" Gilly interrupted, startled. "Why would she kill him? That's just more work for her."

"Good point." I laughed. "But she pings my gut as someone covering up the truth. Whether it's to protect corporate interests or for her own reasons, she stays on the list. And lastly, Ramone."

"Who's Ramone?" Gilly asked, brows raised.

"He's a Latin ballroom dance instructor," I explained. "He came by our table last night to hand out cards." I gestured between Ezra and me. "We saw him cozying up to Callie in the perfumery yesterday afternoon."

"That was the guy?" Gilly threw her hands in the air. "Gah! You miss one dinner, and you miss everything."

"Anyone else?" Pippa asked.

I glanced at Ezra. "Anyone else?"

"You covered it," he said with a smirk. "And then some. The problem is, we have no proof anyone's involved." He rubbed his hands together, eyes twinkling with mischief. "But we're making a Hail Mary play tonight. Who wants to learn some ballroom?"

Everyone raised their hand.

———

DINNER HAD, once again, been delicious. I'd gone for the pork chop with mango salsa this time — the meat tender and juicy, the salsa sweet and tangy with just a hint of heat. The roasted potatoes were buttery and crisp, and the asparagus had a perfect snap. I skipped dessert, though. After the angina scare earlier, I wasn't about to tempt fate with molten chocolate lava cake. No death by dessert tonight.

Afterward, we all went back to change for the ballroom lesson. Ezra pulled on a pair of dark blue pants that hugged his thighs and backside just right, along with a beige shirt that clung to his broad chest and showed off the definition in his arms. He looked good enough to eat.

"Mmm," I said, openly admiring him. "You look better than dinner."

"High praise indeed," he said, grinning. "You're pretty tasty-looking yourself."

"What, this old thing?" I teased, twirling in my black cocktail dress. The bodice dipped low enough to be flirty without crossing into scandalous, and the skirt flared out when I spun, making me feel light and playful.

Ezra caught my hand and pulled me into his arms, spinning me again, this time against his chest.

"Yowza," I purred. "Are you secretly a dancer, Ezra Holden? And if you are, why is this the first I'm hearing about it?"

"I might've done a little West Coast Swing back in my twenties."

My eyes widened. "You're kidding me."

"Not a single bit."

"This will not be the last time you take me out dancing."

He grinned. "Duly noted." He didn't let go of me, holding me close, swaying us to music only he could hear.

"How are you feeling?" he asked softly. Before I could protest, he added, "Just a question. Don't read into it."

"I'm feeling good." And it was the truth. The nitroglycerin earlier had done its job. No more chest pain, no tightness in my neck, no headache, and I wasn't even tired. I patted his chest. "Satisfied?"

He kissed me. "More than."

"And..." I tapped my clutch. "I packed my prescription just in case."

The corners of his eyes softened, the tension easing from his face. "Then I think we have everything we need."

"I couldn't agree more."

I walked to the wall that separated our room from Gilly's and gave it a few good slaps. "Are you all ready?" I called.

"Yep," Gilly shouted back. "I'll check on Pippa."

"I heard you!" Pippa bellowed from two suites away. "We're ready. Meet you in the hall."

Ezra chuckled. "Paper-thin walls."

"Yep," I agreed with a shake of my head. "Paper-thin walls."

Our friends were waiting when we stepped into the hallway, and they looked stunning. Gilly's dress was a fire-engine red sequin number that fit like it had been tailored just for her, and Pippa wore a sleek pearl dress with a thigh slit that screamed Old Hollywood. Jordy had swapped his usual jeans for black slacks and a black button-down shirt with pearl buttons, and the sleeves rolled up just enough to look effortlessly cool. Scott wore charcoal gray pants with an open-collar tuxedo shirt. His eyes stayed locked on Gilly, who was pretending not to notice but was absolutely soaking it up.

Between the six of us, we looked like a group straight out of a heist movie. Three couples dressed to thrill, both figuratively and possibly literally.

Tonight was the night. We were either going to find the killer or force them into a mistake. And if that didn't work, I'd have to take a page from Elsa's playbook and let it go.

The grand ballroom on deck five was just as extravagant as the name promised. Chandeliers sparkled overhead, casting a warm glow over the polished wood floors. The walls were lined with rich, heavy drapes in deep burgundy and gold, adding to the upscale atmosphere. Round tables with neatly pressed white linens sat along the edges of the room.

A grand piano rested in the corner by a main stage, its black surface reflecting the soft lighting, and at the far end, a smaller stage stood ready for live music later in the evening.

When we made our entrance, heads turned. People paused what they were doing to watch us, some whispering, others just staring.

UNFORTUNATELY, it wasn't because we looked like movie stars. It was because we were ridiculously overdressed. The ballroom had listed "cocktail attire" as the dress code, but, apparently, that didn't apply to dance lessons. Most of the other passengers were in cargo shorts, sundresses, and cruise ship merch.

Ah well. I glanced at my friends and shrugged. "I say we own it."

"Damn straight," Gilly said, tossing her chocolate brown hair over her shoulder like a queen.

"Let's light this place on fire," Pippa added, grinning.

Jordy chuckled. "Should we be afraid?"

Scott didn't answer, still too focused on Gilly.

Ezra shook his head slowly, smiling as he took my hand. "No. But everyone else should be."

CHAPTER

# FOURTEEN

"Welcome, welcome, my friends!" Ramone greeted, his voice warm and inviting as more people trickled into the ballroom.

I was pleasantly surprised when Augusta and Carl arrived—I'd missed them at dinner. Even more shocking was the appearance of Helena and Jasper. It was starting to feel like a main dining room reunion special.

At exactly six-thirty, Ramone had the ballroom doors closed and clapped his hands to get everyone's attention. "Tonight," he announced with a flourish, "we will be learning the cha-cha! Now, tell me, does anyone here already know how to cha-cha?"

I nudged Ezra with my elbow. "Well, stud?" I teased. "Do you?"

After learning that he had done West Coast Swing in his twenties, I was both intrigued and annoyed that we hadn't gone dancing before. The thought of watching him in action was more than a little exciting.

"Why don't you show us how it's done, Ezra?" I suggested, grinning.

Gilly caught on immediately. "Yeah, Easy," she chimed in. "Why don't you show us?"

Not to be left out, Pippa added, "Yeah, shake that groove thing!"

I shot her a look. For someone in her thirties, she had a real talent for sounding like a Gen X-er—or even a borderline Boomer—with the way she talked.

Ezra shook his head, smirking. "I don't want to show up the teacher," he said smoothly. "I'll let him demonstrate."

Ramone signaled to someone, and music with a lively, rhythmic beat filled the room. With a microphone clipped to his lapel, he began his lesson. "The cha-cha is danced to four beats," he explained. "You can count it as one, two, three—cha-cha. That's three full beats and two half beats that make up the final four count. And for those of you who are number-challenged," he grinned, "and you know who you are, there's a simpler way to count. Think of it as slow, slow, slow, quick-quick, slow, slow, slow, quick-quick. The slows are full beats, and the quick-quicks are half beats." He smacked his hands together as if dusting them off. "See? Nothing to it."

There were a few laughs and murmurs in the crowd. Ramone was certainly charismatic. I could see why he was popular. I could even see why Callie had been drawn to him.

As he continued to count the beats, he moved his feet effortlessly, his hips swaying with a practiced grace.

"We're going to take this nice and easy," he assured us. "You like it nice and easy, don't you?" He cupped his ear, his feet cha-chaing for the gods, waiting for the crowd's enthusiastic "Yes!"

I leaned against Ezra and murmured, "I'm pretty partial to nice and easy."

He laughed.

Ramone clapped his hands twice at the side of his face like a flamenco dancer. "Everybody now. We are going to go really slow. We're going to do a sidestep to the left for one full beat, then forward one full beat, back on your opposite leg one full beat, then two quick half steps to the right for the final beat. Don't worry if you don't get it right away, just watch my feet, not yours," he added with a grin. "And follow me. Slow, slow, slow, quick-quick. And don't forget the hip action!"

"Yeah, can't forget the hip action," I teased, exchanging a glance with Ezra.

Around the ballroom, guests attempted to follow Ramone's lead with varying levels of success. A few couples actually seemed to have a knack for it, gliding smoothly across the floor with confidence. Others, however, were stumbling through the steps, their movements more frantic than fluid. One woman in a floral maxi dress bumped into her partner and nearly took him down with her. A man in a Hawaiian shirt and khaki shorts moved his feet like he was marching in place, his hips refusing to participate. Poor Pippa wasn't catching on very quickly either. Unlike Shakira, I was pretty sure those hips were lying.

Ezra, on the other hand, was impressive. I mean, I already knew the man had good hip action, but damn. He was really good. He moved with an effortless rhythm, his steps crisp, his posture confident.

"Dang, Easy, get it!" Gilly hooted.

She wasn't so bad herself. I knew she'd taken ballroom lessons for her wedding to Gio a hundred years ago, but my sister from another mister still had it going on. Watching Scott, who was not so graceful, throw caution to the wind and enjoy dancing with her made my angina-racked heart happy.

Augusta and Carl cha-cha'd their way over to us, their movements more steady than flashy.

"You all look so shiny and beautiful," Augusta said, beaming. "Are you going out after the lesson?"

I laughed. "We thought there was a more formal dress code. I read the itinerary wrong."

"I'm glad you did," she said. "You all are the stars of the show."

"We missed you at dinner," I said.

"What?" she asked as the music swelled and the noise level in the room rose.

I leaned in close and repeated, "We missed you at dinner!"

"That's so nice to hear."

As she spoke, a familiar scent drifted toward me. I recognized it instantly. Vertiliance cologne. Callie had hidden the same men's fragrance in her Chanel bag to remind her of her first husband.

Why was I smelling it on Augusta?

*"No," a woman softly cries as she stands near a closed coffin. "Why? Lord, why?" She is wearing a black dress suit and a black hat with a lace fastener. "This is my fault. My fault, my boy. If only I'd kept you. I should've never let you go." Her words drift off. "If only." The regret in her voice is so weighty I can feel it in my chest.*

*Another woman enters, wearing a tightly fitted black dress that hugs her body. She has long auburn hair. "Oh." There is a hint of surprise in her tone. "Do I know you?" I recognize her voice. It's Callie.*

*"No," the other woman says. "But I wanted to come and pay my respects."*

*"How did you know Billy?"*

*"I didn't know him," the woman with the hat says. "Not for a long, long time." She turns to the woman in the fitted dress. "I'm so very sorry for your lo—" Her words are cut short by a choking sob as she rushes past the other woman and mutters, "It didn't have to end this way. It's all my fault."*

*Callie doesn't seem to take notice. She moves closer to the coffin and lays her head down on the smooth mahogany wood. "You promised me," she whispers. "You promised it would always be you and me." She starts to cry, a soul-deep keening that says, My heart is broken into a thousand pieces, and even if it mends, there are some parts that will never be found again.*

My knees buckled when the room came back into view, but Ezra caught me before I collapsed to the floor. My chest, along with my head and neck, felt painfully strained.

"My pills," I managed to say, but Ezra was already digging them out of my clutch.

He placed a tablet under my tongue, and within a minute, the squeezing let up, and the pain faded.

I was crying again, but not because of the angina attack. It had been Billy Grant's funeral, and I'd watched Callie break into pieces the same way my mother had when my dad died. The pain of their grief had been difficult to witness. I couldn't imagine how impossible it was to bear.

"How are you doing?" Ezra asked.

"Fine," I reassured him. "Better."

"Oh, my dear," Augusta said, kneeling next to me. "You scared me half to death."

"Angina attack," I explained. "Apparently, it's my new party trick."

She shook her head but smiled. "At least you still have your sense of humor."

"Sometimes, it's the only thing that gets you through it."

Augusta nodded. "I know the feeling well."

Gilly, Pippa, Scott, and Jordy gathered around me.

"Help her out of the ballroom so she can breathe," Gilly ordered.

"I'm fine," I repeated, though my legs had yet to fully recover.

"You're fine when I tell you you're fine," she snapped.

Damn, I'd really scared her this time.

"I'm sorry, Gils. But, hey, I really am okay. My heart is still working."

"If something happens to you..." She let the implication hang.

"Nothing's going to happen to Nora," Ezra said. "We're not going to let it." He put his arm under mine and looped it around my back for support. "Getting some air is a good idea, though."

His agreeing with Gilly's suggestion gave her a little vindication. I cast him a grateful look.

"What happened?" he asked once we were on the other side of the double doors. "You were talking to Augusta one minute, and the next..." He scrubbed his face. "I've never seen you shake during a vision before. Not like that."

"I know how Augusta and Carl are tied to all this. And I think it might give them one of the biggest motives of all."

I flashed to Gilly asking Augusta and Carl if they had any children, and Carl responding, *Not in this lifetime.* Because her child had been born in another lifetime...one where she'd given him up for adoption.

"Billy Grant was her son," I told Ezra. "Her biological son. She as much as said so in the vision I had of his funeral."

"Well, that wasn't what I expected," he said.

"Expected what?" Gilly asked in a hushed voice.

"That Billy is Augusta's son," Pippa whispered. I guess she'd been close enough to overhear. I looked around to make sure no casuals were nearby.

"What?" Gilly whisper-screamed. "Billy was her son?" She shook her head. "That is a serious motive. If something happened to Marco, God forbid," she crossed herself, "I would straight-up murder that person without an ounce of remorse."

"Agreed," Pippa and Jordy said in unison.

Ezra nodded. "Same. I'd like to think I'd stick to the rule of law, but murder would be more satisfying."

"But wouldn't she blame Callie, not Sebastian?" Pippa mused. "The leaked *fake* recording was persuasive. Until Reese told me it was fake, I believed it."

Jordy put his arm around her. "That's how those deepfakes suck people in. You sell a lie often enough, and even smart people will believe it."

Pippa frowned. "Which still begs the question... why Sebastian and not Callie?"

"Didn't Reese tell you there were rumors that Sebastian was responsible for the terrible emails?" I asked.

"That's true." Pippa put her hands on either side of her head and then mimicked an explosion with them. "This is blowing my mind. But how would Augusta and Carl know about the emails or the fake recording? If not for Reese, we wouldn't have known. It was kept buttoned down and buried."

My legs had finally steadied beneath me. "Well, the Franks are influential. A world-class surgeon and a competent litigator.... You can't tell me they don't know how to get information from even the tightest-lipped sources."

"Even so, I can't see Augusta or Carl as murderers," I admitted, aware I was in complete denial.

Ezra mulled the idea over. "And they might have

killed Callie as well. Two birds. One cruise. Give Callie a shove overboard. Make Sebastian's death look like an unfortunate accident."

The ballroom doors opened, and Helena and Jasper walked through.

"Nora," Helena said. "We were so worried about you. Are you all right?"

She was wearing a sparkly silver tank top with thick straps, but when she turned, I saw something on her right shoulder peeking out from under her strap and through a smudge of makeup used to cover it up.

It was the tattoo. The one from my vision of the young couple on the beach. I narrowed my gaze at her.

"Do you like piña coladas and getting caught in the rain?"

She looked startled but recovered quickly. "Who doesn't?" she replied.

"Nora?" Ezra questioned. "What do you know?"

I knew I had finally placed the shield tattoos I'd seen on the young couple. I'd seen this symbol many times when Ezra went undercover a few years ago.

"You're FBI agents," I finally said. I looked at Jasper.

"How could you know that?" He asked.

"Lucky guess." My voice was flat. "Just like I'm guessing your names aren't really Helena and Jasper Peabody."

Helena was playing it much cooler than Jasper. "What do you think you know, Nora?"

"Only what I'm saying. Were you here investigating Sebastian Caldwell?" I asked point-blank.

"Yes," she answered just as directly. "He'd been blackballed from all the major networks when the rumors circulated about his responsibility in the death of William Grant Jr. But it's one of Hollywood's best-kept secrets. Since then, he's been hemorrhaging money, and he's taken loans out with the Bardonia Syndicate out of Vegas."

"So, Caldwell was broke?"

"Not only broke but flat broke."

That explained why Sebastian and Callie were in the balcony suites instead of the penthouse or the villas.

"Then why bother with him?"

Ezra put his hand on my arm. "To flip him," he explained. "You guys wanted Caldwell to flip on the Baldonias."

"Indeed, we did," Helena confirmed. "When we heard he had some potential investors for a new show outside of the normal channels, we went undercover to get close. We wanted to replace ourselves as the investors, but we couldn't discover who they were and remove them from the cruise in the short time frame. Instead, we had to gain access by proximity. Getting the room across the hall and being assigned to his table was the easiest way to insert ourselves without being too obvious."

I suspected there was more to the "investors" then met the eye. It wasn't a coincidence that Billy Grant's biological mother was at the table with Sebastian and Callie. Had Callie recognized her from the funeral? Is that why Callie couldn't be found? Did they kill her and stash the body somewhere on the ship? Callie would make a convenient scapegoat if anyone looked too closely at the "natural death."

I still didn't want to be sweet, smart, and funny Augusta to be a murderer, but it was the only reason I could think of as to why she smelled like the cologne Callie kept as a reminder of Billy. She'd had to have come in recent contact with Callie...or Callie's body. It made me sick and sad. The world wasn't black and white, and unfortunately, sometimes good people did bad things.

As if my thoughts had conjured her, Augusta exited the ballroom and strolled over to us. Carl was right behind her, and he looked upset.

"Are you okay, Nora?" She gave me a sympathetic smile. "You gave me quite a scare in there when you had that seizure."

It wasn't a seizure, but I could see how seeing me mid-vision could look like one. "I'm okay," I told her. I glanced at Helena. "But I don't think you will be."

She tucked her chin, and her eyes crinkled. "What do you mean?" There was something about the shape of them, the way they dipped at the corners...something I hadn't noticed before. I couldn't put my finger on it, though. In the end, I'm not sure it mattered.

"You arranged the trip to get Sebastian and Callie on the cruise, didn't you?"

The question startled her. "Whatever do you mean?"

"What are you talking about, Nora?" Helena asked. "Why would Augusta do that?" She frowned then looked at the older woman. "Are you and Carl the investors?"

Augusta shook her head. "It wasn't..." She clenched her eyes shut them opened them. "This wasn't supposed to happen."

"I am completely lost," Jasper said. "Someone explain it to me."

"Augusta is Billy Grant's biological mother."

Carl let out an angry grunt. "How dare—"

Augusta held a hand up to silence his denials. "I gave birth to Billy Grant," she admitted.

Rebecca Hansen showed up. "What's going on? I got a call there was a commotion in the ballroom. A passenger passed out or something."

"It was me," I told her. "I'm fine now."

She narrowed her gaze at Augusta then Helena. "Is there something going on I should know about?"

"Sebastian's death wasn't an accident or natural causes." I stared at her, daring her to tell me to stay out of it one more time. "And I don't care what the cruise line wants you to do to avoid a scandal or a full-scale investigation."

Ezra backed me up. "Caldwell didn't get in that pool by himself. He was dragged there on a lounge chair and pushed into the water."

"I'm the authority on this boat," Hansen said. Her expression was determined. "I don't have to discuss the investigation or its conclusions with you. And I've about had enough of your interference."

Helena reached into her handbag and pulled out her identification. "I think we'll take over from here," she informed Hansen. "Lynn Maigret, FBI."

Jasper took his wallet out and opened it, flashing his badge. "Paul Maigret, FBI."

"I did it," Augusta confessed. "I killed Sebastian Caldwell. I killed Callie, too."

"Augusta," Carl said sharply. "No!"

She put her hand on his cheek. "This is the right thing to do."

He kissed her palm, and she closed her eyes for a moment, tears leaking from her eyes. "I don't want anyone innocent getting blamed for something I made happen."

Hansen looked surprised. "Well, uhm, this changes things." She shook her head. "Sorry, Nora, I really thought..."

Augusta turned to me, and unexpectedly, she hugged me, as a stream of moments from her past flooded quickly through my mind. It was as if her life were flashing before my eyes. From giving birth, to meeting Carl, to passing the bar exam, and it went on. None of them lasted long enough for me to grab onto one thing, and when Augusta let me go, they were gone.

In the years since my gift manifested, I'd never experienced anything like it. I looked at Augusta. She smiled at me. "It was so nice meeting you, Nora."

Hansen was practically vibrating as she nodded to the FBI couple. "You can use my office if you want."

Lynn, formerly known as Helena, said, "We'd be grateful for the space. Do you have handcuffs?"

Hansen took her cuffs out and handed them over. Paul, formerly known as Jasper, took them and placed them on Augusta's wrists and read her the Miranda rights."

"Augusta," I called out, certain now she was covering for someone. "Don't talk without a lawyer."

Augusta might've thought she was doing something noble—something to pay back her son for giving him up all those years ago—but losing the life she'd built with Carl for crimes she didn't commit would be more punishment than either of them deserved.

"I am a lawyer," she replied as Lynn, Paul, and Hansen escorted her to the elevator.

"What did you see, Nora?" Ezra asked when they were out of earshot.

"Enough to know that Augusta is not a murderer. I'm pretty sure I know who is, though." The pieces were falling into place. "We need to expose the real killer before we hit Cozumel. And I've got an idea of where to start."

# FIFTEEN

When I explained the plan to everyone, I got a few *"Are you out of your mind?"* comments...mostly from Gilly, who was still pissed at me for scaring her with my heart problems.

Ezra was a rockstar, though. He supported the plan, as long as we stuck together. I was good with that. Going off on my own was a really good way to get my butt kicked—something I'd experienced a time or two in the course of my work with the police. I didn't want any gunshot wounds, broken bones, or black eyes.

Of course, for the plan to really work, we'd need the FBI to give us an assist. I left that task up to Pippa. She could be very convincing. I offered Gilly an out. Neither Scott nor she was obligated to participate in what she called a *"harebrained plan."* That's when she called me a harebrain and told me it would be a cold day in hell before she let me out of her sight. Scott wasn't going to let Gilly out of *his* sight, and so, our scouting team became a party of four.

Before heading out, we changed into less formal, more stealthy, stretchy clothes. Tight dresses and heels weren't exactly ideal for sneaking around the ship.

"How do we sneak into the morgue?" Gilly asked as we took the elevator down to the second floor.

If I was right, the real murderer would come down here soon while the FBI was occupied with getting the details of Augusta's questions and try to get rid of Sebastian's body. If it were to go over the rail and disappear into the ocean...well....no body, no crime. Or, at least, it would be hard to prove. Augusta was a smart enough lawyer to know that confessions can be overturned. People already suspected the young singer had jumped over the rail. On top of that, no body, no autopsy to prove that he hadn't died of natural causes.

"Scott, since you're a doctor, can you fake an emergency to distract whoever's on duty tonight?" I requested.

"Easy enough," he said, but I could tell it made him uncomfortable.

"I'll do it," Gilly said, sensing it as well.

"No," he said firmly. "I'm part of this Scooby gang now, and I'm going to do my part."

"You dear, sweet man," I gushed. "I could totally kiss you."

My statement drew objections from both Ezra and Gilly.

"I meant metaphorically." I rolled my eyes. "Dude?"

"Dude," she replied.

I blew out a breath. "Duude."

"Duuude." Gilly put her hands on her hips.

"Duuuude." I widened my eyes for emphasis.

She nodded. "Dude."

I smiled. "Dude." We were cool again.

"You guys are so strange sometimes," Ezra said.

To which Gilly and I both said, "Duuuuuude," then laughed.

I knew the levity was a result of nervous energy. We both resorted to humor in times of stress. Well, humor *or* wanting to punch someone's ticket. I was glad that we'd decided not to choose violence. Humor was a much better option.

"We'll hang back by the elevators until Scott creates the distraction. And while they're busy with him, we'll slip down the restricted corridor to the morgue."

"Bulletproof," Gilly said with only a hint of sarcasm. I was calling that progress. "How do we know which drawer to look in?"

"There can't be that many." I dipped my chin. "We'll search them all."

"Wonderful," she mumbled.

Ezra held a hand up to shush us as the elevator stopped and the doors opened. "Keep out of sight."

"But make sure the cameras see us," I added.

"Harebrained," Gilly reiterated.

"You're on," Ezra told his golfing pal.

Scott nodded, clutched his side and staggered to the clinic door. "Help," rasped out, before letting out a low, miserable groan. "I think...it's my appendix." His face was twisted in pain, and honestly, if I didn't know better, I'd be worried.

Nurse Tony, the same tall nurse who had used the defibrillator on Sebastian the night before, was once again on the night shift. He immediately stepped forward, his expression shifting from boredom to concern. "Let's get you inside," he said, wrapping an arm around Scott's back to help him through the door.

Scott moaned again, perfectly timing the fake agony. He knew exactly when the pain was supposed to spike and just how bad it should be getting. As the clinic door shut behind them, Ezra motioned for us to move.

We slipped past the clinic, keeping close to the wall, our steps light and quick. I held my breath as we passed the doorway, every muscle in my body tense. As we were almost clear of the clinic, I heard Nurse Tony say, "We may need a surgeon."

Crap.

Gilly flashed me a "my husband better not come back to me with any missing parts" look.

I grimaced, then shrugged. I knew Scott was willing to take one for the team, but surgery was going several steps too far. My stomach twisted with guilt. We'd joked about distractions, but I didn't actually want him to end up under the knife.

I had to trust, though, that Scott wouldn't let it get that far...no matter how much he wanted to impress us.

We moved quickly and quietly down the dimly lit corridor, the hum of the ship's ventilation system masking the sound of our footsteps. The metal door to the morgue was tucked away at the end of the hall, blending in with the surrounding walls except for a small access panel and a heavy-duty handle. It looked industrial, utilitarian, none of the polished, flashy elegance the rest of the ship had. Just cold, gray steel, a little scuffed near the edges where it had seen years of use.

A 360-degree security camera sat mounted on the ceiling just outside the door. I glanced up at it, noting the dark, lifeless lens. "Disabled," I muttered, not surprised. I had a feeling the one at the Resplendent Retreat had been purposefully disabled as well. Still, just for kicks, I flipped it the bird.

The door was thankfully wedged open slightly. The person using it wouldn't want to be caught swiping in an out multiple times a day. We slipped inside.

The morgue was about as inviting as you'd expect. Cold steel everything, a few rolling carts, and a wall lined with freezer drawers. The air was crisp enough to make my breath fog, and the scent of disinfectant barely covered the underlying metallic tang. Fluorescent lights buzzed overhead, casting a harsh glow that somehow made everything look even more unsettling.

Gilly shivered and wrapped her arms around herself. "Well," she said, "this isn't creepy at all."

I smirked. "Just wait until the corpses start singing *The Monster Mash*."

She snorted. "That's how we'll know they're cool."

"Let's just get this over with before Scott ends up

actually needing a surgeon," Ezra said, rubbing his hands together for warmth.

"There are only twelve drawers," I said, scanning them. "Shouldn't take long."

"How do we know which one is the right one?" Gilly asked.

Ezra glanced at the wall, then at me. "Open them all up until we find Sebastian."

Gilly raised an eyebrow. "What if there are other dead people in there?"

I shook my head. "If it's not Sebastian then move on to the next drawer."

I opened three drawers on the right, starting at the top, when I went to open the fourth, I heard Ezra say," Got him."

I was already sliding the drawer out, and saw it wasn't empty like the others. Oh, crap. On top of that, it wasn't quite as chilled as the others.

"I think you all need to come see this," I told them, gripping the handle. I slid the drawer all the way out, bracing myself for what we might find.

It was the last thing I expected to see.

Instead, of a dead body, a pair of sleepy eyes stared up at me.

Alive.

"It's Callie," I said breathlessly.

Gilly whispered, "No freaking way."

The ex-reality star-slash-widow twice over was bundled up under a thermal heating blanket, the kind with an extra battery pack attached. A small oxygen mask covered her nose and mouth, the attached tank nestled near the outer edge of the drawer. Two unopened bottles of water sat beside her. Whoever had put her here hadn't meant for her to die. Not immediately, anyway. They had wanted her alive, just barely.

Her body was still curled up in the fetal position, as if trying to conserve every bit of warmth. Her fingers clutched the edges of the blanket, her knuckles white. Even with the heating pack, she was shivering, her breaths coming shallow and quick through the mask.

"Callie?"

Her eyes widened at the sound of her name, blinking sluggishly against the light.

"Is it time to go?" she mumbled sleepily, her voice muffled by the mask.

"Yes," I told her. "You're safe now. It's time to go home."

Panic flickered across her face, her muscles tensing as if she were about to fight. Then, recognition hit.

"Nora?" Her voice was barely a whisper.

"Yeah, it's me," I said, trying to keep my voice steady. "You're safe now."

Gilly exhaled sharply. "I can't believe it. I can't believe she's actually alive."

"Not so harebrained now, am I?" Although finding Callie alive hadn't been on my list of things I thought I'd discover tonight. Instead, it was a happy accident.

Ezra reached in, checking the oxygen tank, his movements quick and efficient. "She's stable, but we need to get her out of here now."

I placed a hand on the young woman's arm, squeezing gently. "Can you move?"

She nodded weakly, her fingers twitching against the blanket. "Help me," she groaned.

"I will," I said, sliding an arm under her and preparing to lift. "Let's get the hell out of here."

"What about Sebastian?" Gilly asked. "We have to move his body, right?"

"Moving Callie to a safe location takes priority," Ezra said.

With our backs to the door, we hadn't noticed it was closing until it slammed shut.

I whipped around and saw exactly who I thought I'd see. "Hello, Rebecca."

Security Chief Hansen stood inside the room with us, a taser in one hand and a flare gun in the other.

Ezra raised a brow at the selection. "A flare gun?"

"They keep track of bullets," she stated.

"Ah," he said. "Makes sense."

"You don't have to do this," I told her.

"But I do," she said. Her downturned eyes were wide as she kept us covered. The shape of them made her look almost doll-like "It's for my..." Her words trailed off. "I won't explain myself to you."

"You don't have to explain anything," I said. "I know why you've done this."

When Augusta had hugged me, I'd seen the truth of Billy's birth. He hadn't come into the world alone. And looking at Rebecca Hansen's face when she was next to Augusta, I could see the resemblance in not only the shape of her eyes, but in the fullness of her lips and her high cheekbones. The family resemblance was there.

"You're Billy Grant's twin, and Augusta is your mother"

Rebecca's face went pale. "How did you... how could you... how—" she sputtered.

"I knew there had to be a reason Augusta was taking the blame for killing Sebastian and Callie. I might've believed her killing the man responsible for pushing Billy over the edge, but Callie? Augusta knew how much she loved Billy, how his death had shattered her from the inside out. She'd seen it firsthand at Billy's funeral." I shook my head. "I didn't believe for one second that she killed the girl."

Rebecca's expression was filled with the desperation of someone in way over her head. She looked like she wanted an out.

"You have your mother's eyes," I said gently.

Her face twisted. "You don't understand," she pleaded. "I didn't..."

Gilly tried reasoning with her. "I'm really sorry for all the bad that's happened to you. To your brother." She put herself between Rebecca and Callie. "But killing that terrible man wasn't going to bring him back."

"No," a voice rasped behind my friend. "But it brought me so much joy."

I pivoted, just in time to see Callie raising the oxygen tank up high, aiming for Gilly's head.

"Look out!" I yelled.

Gilly ducked the blow just in time, slamming her

elbow into Callie's gut. At the same moment, Ezra launched himself at Rebecca. The taser came loose from her hand and slid across the floor as they went down.

Gilly and Callie were on the ground now, both wrestling for control in a tangle of limbs, rolling across the tile as Callie clawed and thrashed, fighting like hell. Ezra and Rebecca struggled as well. She was taller, well-trained, and dangerous. But Ezra was a skilled fighter, too. He managed to pin one of her arms, but she twisted, leveraging her weight, and suddenly, he was the one flat on his back.

I snatched up the taser, my hands shaky but unwavering. Ezra had let me shoot one into a dummy once at their training facility. This wasn't a dummy.

Rebecca's hand went for Ezra's throat.

I didn't hesitate.

Fifty thousand volts shot through her, the charge locking up her muscles as she went rigid. She spasmed and collapsed sideways, her body still twitching.

Ezra scrambled to his feet.

"Help Gilly," I pleaded. "I got this one."

About the time they had Callie—who turned out to be hella scrappy—under control, FBI agents Paul and Lynn Maigret came bursting through the door.

"What the heck happened in here?" Lynn said, taking in the chaotic scene. Then her gaze dropped onto Callie. "Oh my gosh," she muttered. "She's alive. She's still alive."

"Uhm, yeah," I said, taking the lead with Lynn while

Ezra helped Paul restrain the two women and read them their rights. Gilly ran out to check on Scott.

"What can you tell me?"

"I'm fuzzy on a lot of the details, but I'm fairly certain Callie killed Sebastian, and Rebecca moved the body, and I'm really confused by what they planned to do when we arrived in Cozumel, but I think Hansen was going to offload her with her husband's corpse."

"And Augusta Frank?" Helena asked. What's her role in all this?"

My brow pinched between my eyes. "Just a woman who wanted to be a good mom, but it was too little too late."

"What are you, a middle-aged Spiderwoman?" the female FBI agent asked. "You have one heck of a developed spidey sense. I couldn't hardly believe it when your friend told me what you were up to. When I wouldn't get on board, she tried to make me believe you were some kind of psychic." She scoffed. "As if."

My smile felt feral as I looked down at her wedding rings and said, "Where's the pear-shaped diamond your husband gave you when you got engaged?"

"How? What? Oh my gosh." She held out her hand and looked at the rings. "The real engagement ring cost Paul almost a year's salary. I don't wear it when we're undercover." She gave me an assessing stare. "How in the world did you know?"

I touched my nose. "I have a gift."

"And a curse," Gilly said.

"And a gift," I added. To Lynn, I asked, "What will happen to Augusta?"

She shrugged. "It depends on her part in all this, but I hope she doesn't see any jail time. I liked her."

I nodded. "I liked her too."

---

AFTER THE ARREST of Rebecca Hansen and Callie Caldwell for the murder of Sebastian Caldwell—a pig and a real piece of crap, but still a human being—Augusta admitted to hatching a scheme to get revenge on him. Poor Carl loved her so much that he went along with the crazy scam. The plan was to bilk Sebastian out of what little money he had left, leaving him destitute and desperate. Killing him hadn't been part of the program.

With the help of her biological daughter, whom she'd reconnected with a few years back, Augusta set the wheels of tragedy in motion. What they hadn't accounted for was the fact that Callie had been living like an ostrich since Billy died—head in the sand and high on benzodiazepines most of the time. And when she finally woke up and realized that the man she'd been sharing her bed with had tortured and tormented the love of her life in her name, she'd completely lost it.

She said she'd seen one of the maintenance men with rat poison, and she'd never known a bigger rat than Sebastian. Using a little sleight of hand, she'd picked up working at an opening act for a third-rate magician when she was a teenager. She'd brazenly snuck pellets of

163

rat poison into the olives in front of the whole table when she was putting them on his plate from her salad.

"He inhaled the olives without even chewing," Callie had told the FBI agents. "He made it so easy."

By the time Sebastian started feeling the effects, it had been too late for him. The poison had zinc phosphide in it, a coagulant that poisoned him quickly and had an added side effect of elevating his platelets.

Once he was dead, Rebecca felt she had little choice but to cover the whole thing up. She knew the cruise company was notorious for listing any death, not obviously murder, as an accident or natural causes—saved them a lot of legal hassle. All she had to do was get Sebastian and Callie off the boat without anyone looking too closely.

But they hadn't seen us coming.

Charise's presence had been a coincidence. The ill-treated songbird decided to quit the cruise line and find a place where she could enjoy anonymity once more. Ramone, it turned out, hadn't been having an affair with Callie. What we'd seen in the perfumery had been nothing more than some harmless flirting.

With the investigation behind us, we jumped head-first back into our planned sun, fun, and no more murder.

We got off the boat in Cozumel in the morning. Gilly and Scott did their adventure dive, Jordy and Pippa snorkeled with the turtles, and Ezra and I—well, we parasailed. Ezra was concerned about my heart, but I managed to get through the whole terrifying thing without any angina attacks. I'm calling it a win.

Did I enjoy parasailing? Absolutely not.

Am I glad I did it? Nope. Not even a little.

Would I do it again? If Ezra asked me? Yeah. Probably.

He would do anything for me, and in turn, I would do the same for him. Love went both ways, and he proved every day he was a man I could trust with my heart, damaged or otherwise. After Augusta, Carl, Callie, and Rebecca were removed from the ship, I didn't have one single chest pain again. Not even a twinge. I promised Gilly, Pippa, and Ezra I'd see a cardiologist when we got back home, but I had a feeling my angina had been a side effect of the broken-hearted visions. Only time would tell. Until then, I wasn't going to let fear make decisions for me.

On the last night of the cruise, we watched the final sunset with our friends. Other than the first two days, the whole vacation had been magical. Ezra took me dancing, and I hadn't had that much fun on two feet in forever. Of course, my legs were sore the following day, but it had been worth it. Now that I knew my guy could dance, I planned to make it a regular date.

As we cuddled in bed, I knew I'd hit the life-lottery jackpot.

I had a great life with fulfilling work, loyal-to-then-end friends, and a wonderful man who loved me.

I met his sleepy gaze.

"Thank you," I said.

He smiled. "For what?"

"You always ask me that."

He shrugged, his thumb brushing over my knuckles. "I like hearing your answers."

"Thank you for teaching me what it means to have a real partner." I kissed his neck. "Thank you for loving me so well."

His throat bobbed as he swallowed hard. He kissed me, his lips warm and soft as they moved against mine. When he finally spoke, his voice was rough with emotion. "Sometimes I think that's what I was put on this earth for, Nora. Just to love you."

My eyes stung as tears clouded my vision. "You're going to make me cry," I whispered.

He kissed me again. "Because you're happy."

"Because I'm happy," I confirmed, my voice barely above a breath.

And I was.

THE END

PREORDER BOOK *11 in the Nora Black Series, Lime and Punishment*

**When Nora is tasked with judging a key lime pie eating contest, one of the contestants is left pucker-faced when he dies mid-bite. Was it an accidental death, an act of sabotage gone wrong? Or was it fresh-squeezed murder?**

Nora Black and her nose are on the case, and her visions are sweet, sour, and tart enough to sour a killer's plan.

# PIT PERFECT MURDER
## BARKSIDE OF THE MOON COZY MYSTERIES
## BOOK 1

**Chapter 1 - Sneak Peek**

**When I was eighteen years** old, I came home from a sleepover and found my mom and dad with their throats cut, and their hearts ripped from their chests.

My little brother Danny was in a broom closet in the kitchen, his arms wrapped around his knees, and his face pale and ghostly. Until that day, I'd planned to go to college and study medicine after graduation, but instead, I ended up staying home and taking care of my seven-year-old brother.

Seventeen years later, my brother was murdered. At the time, Danny's death looked like it would go unsolved, much like my parents' had.

Without Haze Kinsey, my best friend since we were five, the killers would have gotten away with it. She was a special agent for the FBI for almost a decade, and when I called her about Danny's death, she dropped everything to come help me get him justice. The evil group of witches and Shifters responsible for the decimation of my family paid with their lives.

Yes. I said witches and Shifters. Did I forget to mention I'm a werecougar? Oh, and my friend Hazel is a witch. Recently, I discovered witches in my own family tree on my mother's side. Shifters, in general, only mated with Shifters, but witches were the exception. As a matter of fact, my friend Haze is mated to a bear Shifter.

I wouldn't have known about the witch in my genealogy, though, if a rogue witch coven hadn't done some funky hoodoo witchery to me. Apparently, the spell activated a latent talent that had been dormant in my hybrid genes.

My ancestor's magic acted like truth serum to anyone who came near her. No one could lie in her presence. Lucky me, my ability was a much lesser form of hers. People didn't have to tell me the truth, but whenever they were around me, they had the compulsion to overshare all sorts of private matters about themselves. This can get seriously uncomfortable for all parties involved. Like, the fact that I didn't need to know that Janet Strickland had been wearing the same pair of underwear for an entire week, or that Mike Dandridge had sexual fantasies about clowns.

My newfound talent made me unpopular and unwelcome in a town full of paranormal creatures who thrived on little deceptions. So, when Haze discovered the whereabouts of my dad's brother, a guy I hadn't known even existed, I sold all my belongings, let the bank have my parents' house, jumped in my truck, and headed south.

After two days and 700 miles of nonstop gray, snowy weather, I pulled my screeching green and yellow mini-truck into an auto repair shop called The Rusty Wrench. Much like my beloved pickup, I'd needed a new start, and moving to a small town occupied by humans seemed the best shot. I'd barely made it to Moonrise, Missouri before my truck began its death throes. The vehicle protested the last 127 miles by sputtering to a halt as I rolled her into the closest spot.

The shop was a small white-brick building with a one-car garage off to the right side. A black SUV and a white compact car occupied two of the six parking spots.

A sign on the office door said: *No Credit Cards. Cash Only. Some Local Checks Accepted (Except from Earl—You Know Why, Earl! You check-bouncing bastard).*

A man in stained coveralls, wiping a greasy tool with a rag, came out the side door of the garage. He had a full head of wavy gray hair, bushy eyebrows over light blue, almost colorless eyes, and a minimally lined face that made me wonder about his age. I got out of the truck to greet him.

"Can I help you, miss?" His voice was soft and raspy with a strong accent that was not quite Deep South.

"Yes, please." I adjusted my puffy winter coat. "The heater stopped working first. Then the truck started jerking for the last fifty miles or so."

He scratched his stubbly chin. "You could have

thrown a rod, sheared the distributor, or you have a bad ignition module. That's pretty common on these trucks."

I blinked at him. I could name every muscle in the human body and twelve different kinds of viruses, but I didn't know a spark plug from a radiator cap. "And that all means..."

"If you threw a rod, the engine is toast. You'll need a new vehicle."

"Crap." I grimaced. "What if it's the other thingies?"

The scruffy mechanic shrugged. "A sheared distributor is an easy fix, but I have to order in the part, which means it won't get fixed for a couple of days. Best-case scenario, it's the ignition module. I have a few on hand. Could get you going in a couple of hours, but..." he looked over my shoulder at the truck and shook his head, "...I wouldn't get your hopes up."

I must've looked really forlorn because the guy said, "It might not need any parts. Let me take a look at it first. You can grab a cup of coffee across the street at Langdon's One-Stop."

He pointed to the gas station across the road. It didn't look like much. The pale-blue paint on the front of the building looked in need of a new coat, and the weather-beaten sign with the store's name on it had seen better days. There was a car at the gas pumps and a couple more in the parking lot, but not enough to call it busy.

I'd had enough of one-stops, though, thank you. The bathrooms had been horrible enough to make a wereraccoon yark, and it took a lot to make those garbage eaters sick. Besides, I wasn't just passing through Moonrise, Missouri.

"Have you ever heard of The Cat's Meow Café?" Saying the name out loud made me smile the way it had when Hazel had first said it to me. I'd followed my GPS into town, so I knew I wasn't too far away from the place.

"Just up the street about two blocks, take a right on Sterling Street. You can't miss it. I should have some news in about an hour or so, but take your time."

"Thank you, Mister…"

"Greer." He shoved the tool in his pocket. "Greer Knowles."

"I'm Lily Mason."

"Nice to meet ya," said Greer. "The place gets hoppin' around noon. That's when church lets out."

I looked at my phone. It was a little before noon now. "Good. I could go for something to eat. How are the burgers?"

"Best in town," he quipped.

I laughed. "Good enough."

Even in the sub-freezing temperature, my hands were sweating in my mittens. I wasn't sure what had me more nervous, leaving the town I grew up in for the first time in my life or meeting an uncle I'd never known existed.

I crossed a four-way intersection. One of the signs was missing, and I saw the four-by-four post had snapped off at its base. I hadn't noticed it on my way in. Crap. Had I run a stop sign? I walked the two blocks to Sterling. The diner was just where Greer had said. A blue truck, a green mini-coup, and a sheriff's SUV were parked out front.

An alarm dinged as the glass door opened to The Cat's Meow. Inside, there was a row of six booths along the wall, four tables that seated four out in the open floor, and counter seating with about eight cushioned black stools. The interior décor was rustic country with orange tabby kitsch everywhere. A man in blue jeans and a button-down shirt with a string tie sat in the nearest booth. A female police officer sat at a counter chair sipping coffee and eating a cinnamon roll. Two elderly women, one with snowball-white hair, the other a dyed strawberry-blonde, sat in a back booth.

The white poof-headed lady said, "This egg is not over-medium."

"Well, call the mayor," said Redhead. "You're unhappy with your eggs. Again."

"See this?" She pointed at the offending egg. "Slime, right here. Egg snot. You want to eat it?"

"If it'll make you shut up about breakfast food, I'll eat it and lick the plate."

A man with copper-colored hair and a thick beard, tall and well-muscled, stepped out of the kitchen. He wore a white apron around his waist, and he had on a black T-shirt and blue jeans. He held a plate with a single fried egg shining in the middle.

The old woman with the snowy hair blushed, her thin skin pinking up as he crossed the room to their table. "Here you go, Opal. Sorry 'bout the mix-up on your egg." He slid the plate in front of her. "This one is pure perfection." He grinned, his broad smile shining. "Just like you." He winked.

Opal giggled.

The redhead rolled her eyes. "You're as easy as the eggs."

"Oh, Pearl. You're just mad he didn't flirt with you."

As the women bickered over the definition of flirting, the cook glanced at me. He seemed startled to see me there. "You can sit anywhere," he said. "Just pick an open spot."

"I'm actually looking for someone," I told him.

"Who?"

"Daniel Mason." Saying his name gave me a hollow ache. My parents had named my brother Daniel, which told me my dad had loved his brother, even if he didn't speak about him.

The man's brows rose. "And why are you looking for him?"

I immediately knew he was a werecougar like me. The scent was the first clue, and his eyes glowing, just for a second, was another. "You're Daniel Mason, aren't you?"

He moved in closer to me and whispered barely audibly, but with my Shifter senses, I heard him loud and clear. "I go by Buzz these days."

"Who's your new friend, Buzz?" the policewoman asked. Now that she was looking up from her newspaper, I could see she was young.

He flashed a charming smile her way. "Never you mind, Nadine." He gestured to a waitress, a middle-aged woman with sandy-colored hair, wearing a black T-shirt and a blue jean skirt. "Top off her coffee, Freda. Get Nadine's mind on something other than me."

"That'll be a tough 'un, Buzz." Freda laughed. "I don't think Deputy Booth comes here for the cooking."

"More like the cook," the elderly lady with the light strawberry-blonde hair said. She and her friend cackled.

The policewoman's cheeks turned a shade of crimson that flattered her chestnut-brown hair and pale complexion. "Y'all mind your P's and Q's."

Buzz chuckled and shook his head. He turned his attention back to me. "Why is a pretty young thing like you interested in plain ol' me?"

I detected a slight apprehension in his voice.

"If you're Buzz Mason, I'm Lily Mason, and you're my uncle."

The man narrowed his dark-emerald gaze at me. "I think we'd better talk in private."

**Keep Reading!**

# YOU'VE GOT TAIL
## PECULIAR MYSTERIES & ROMANCES BOOK 1

### Chapter One

**SOME PEOPLE JUMP** into the deep end of the pool feet first, some head first, but I've always been a traditional belly-flopper. Splashy, messy, and usually painful. Which still didn't explain why I was sitting on the floor of a closed diner, nursing my bruised butt, not to mention my pride, and staring woefully at a naked unconscious man in the middle of Peculiar, Missouri.

My parents are crazy from way back. Maybe that's where I get it from. Seriously, who names a child Ambrosia Sunshine? Two hippies, that's who. They told me when I was old enough to resent the flower child name that they'd thought it was cool at the time, but I personally believe it was the result of one too many 'shrooms. As it is, I've been forced to sit through many painful renditions of "You Are My Sunshine." If I had a dead body for every time I was teased, well, let's just say I'd get an express pass to the electric chair. Although, if I got a sympathetic judge, he'd probably consider my life-time served.

Maybe my parents' experimentation with drugs is what had made me psychic. (No, I didn't say psychotic. I said *psychic*.) On the other hand, it could also explain why I'm so bad at it.

My ability allows me glimpses, more like screen-shots, of the past, present, and future. But, clearly, the visions have *not* been helpful over the years. And the side effects, sheesh. Most of the time I feel a little dizzy when they hit, but every once in a while, it's as if someone has taken a sledgehammer to the inside of my skull. Usually, I can feel one coming on; otherwise driving might be an issue. If only they made medic-alert bracelets for my type of ailment. It certainly hasn't been a gift.

That's why my friendship with Chavvah Trimmel is so important. We'd met at the community college in San Diego. She thought my name was weird and awesome all rolled up into a spring roll. After finding out her family's propensity for strange biblical names, I thought it was a bit of the pot calling the kettle rusty. Chavvah, or Chav, as she likes to be called, was my first best friend. And when she's around me, my psychic mojo kicks up twenty notches. It's as if I can tap into some kind of mystic hotline whenever she's near.

As a matter of fact, the last time I'd gotten a clear vision had been in my dining room back in California.

Chav, who'd been renting my spare bedroom at the time, had just turned down the heat on the spaghetti sauce, and I was setting the table. We were having an "I finally dumped the cheating bastard" celebratory dinner. Did I mention I'm a bad psychic? So I hadn't a clue what I was walking in on when I caught my boyfriend of three years having sex with the skank waitress from the coffee shop. On my couch, no less. Jerk. I took his spare key and kicked his ass (and the couch) to the curb.

At dinner that night, when the vision hit me, I'd hit the ground, along with some clattering dishes. I saw a present moment of Chav's parents huddled together, debating whether to call her about her missing brother. Talk about being the bearer of bad news. I didn't blame her for not believing me at first, or the stunned look she gave me when she called her parents, and it turned out to be true. Her brother Judah had dropped off the map.

Chav flew back to Missouri the next day. After a year of searching for him, the local police had pretty much given up on Judah, but by that time, Chav had forgotten about the ocean and fallen in love with the little town of Peculiar. Hell, from her letters and phone calls, I'd kind of fallen in love with the place as well. She'd found a restaurant in the rural town, a real fixer-upper, for the two of us to run. A fifty-fifty partner split.

I wasn't supposed to leave California for another two weeks, and Chav had said she needed to talk to me "in person" before I made the trip, but the text I'd gotten from her had sent me packing in a hurry.

All it said was: *Sunny. I need u.*

After that, every call I'd made to Chav went straight to voice mail. Without any real plan, I jumped into my gas-guzzling Toyota 4X4, which I had purchased explicitly for the move. One thousand six hundred and sixty-two point four miles later, as I drove over a swinging bridge (the only way in and out, I soon discovered) into the quaint little town, my whole body heaved a sigh of relief. I felt strangely wonderful. It was as if someone unzipped my off-the-rack skin and fitted me with a tailored Sunny suit.

The town looked very similar to Mayberry from *The Andy Griffith Show*. Dirt streets, old fashioned shops and houses, white picket fences, and lots of Chevy and Ford pickup trucks. I was a little nervous when my GPS said, "You have arrived," right outside a two-story yellow building on the corner of Third Street and Main.

My heart pounded as I stood outside our restaurant for the first time. I'd always expected some kind of fanfare. Chav waiting to usher me into our future. She'd even named the restaurant for me. Sunny's Outlook. I'd blame allergies for my eyes watering at that moment, but I knew it was a mixture of happiness and sadness all rolled into one big bundle. This was *our* place. Mine and Chav's. And she'd done it up spectacularly.

I smiled at the brightly colored lettering. All the letters except the big O in Outlook were blue. The O was not an O at all, but a bright orange sun. If it was possible to feel both warm and cold at the same time, I accomplished it.

Where was Chav? I knew in my bones something was wrong. The year we'd spent apart had dulled my psychic ability toward her, so once again I had become inept with crazy flashes that didn't amount to much of anything.

I jiggled the door handle. It wasn't locked, so being the smart, city-savvy girl I am, I decided to let myself in. After all, I owned half the joint, so I wasn't trespassing.

Darkness enclosed the front room except a few areas illuminated by sunlight filtering into the two small windows near the ceiling. They were surrounded by open wooden shutters. Where were the large storefront windows? This place was more dive bar than restaurant. Strange decor choice but my concern for Chav kept me from imagining a complete makeover. I couldn't find a light switch around the door. I should have just gone back out to the truck for a flashlight, but I thought I saw a panel on the wall across the room, and frankly, it was sheer laziness that moved me forward.

I managed to maneuver around the counter, open the panel, and flicked several of the switches at once. The lights came on and when I stepped back to admire my new home lit up—it didn't look half bad; hardwood floors, cute little tables with black-and-white gingham cloth, and a couple of booths with the same checkered design on the benches.

And that's when it happened. My heel caught on something large, and I fell ass-backward to the ground. It didn't take more than a nanosecond to see that I'd tripped over a naked man passed out cold on the floor.

After a startled yelp, heart palpitations, and worry that he'd wake up at any moment and kill me, I reached over and touched him. Just his arm, mind you. He didn't move, but his skin felt warm, and his chest raised and lowered, so I didn't bother to check for a pulse.

Instead, I found myself staring...for several minutes. (Come on. He was naked and lying on his back. Who wouldn't stare?) Dark-brown hair populated his broad chest and led to a happy trail that, well, if the circumstances had been different would have made me very happy indeed. He had thickly muscled thighs and arms, and his face, except for the scruffy five o'clock shadow, looked as if it had been chiseled by Michelangelo. Imagine a better-looking Wolverine (Hugh Jackman's version), but much younger and with a burly lumberjack vibe, and coarse, medium-length walnut-brown hair.

I chewed my lower lip as I took my time pondering the situation—in other words, I wasn't ready to stop staring at the naked man. His hair was near the same hue of brown as my own, when it wasn't dyed blonde, which was never. And mine was shorter with a better haircut. I sighed with regret. I already missed my stylist in California.

Taking a deep breath, I counted backward from ten to pull myself out of the hormonal frenzy going on in my head. The man was hotter than a habanero, but I wasn't looking for a date. I smelled a pungent sweet scent I hadn't noticed before, but frankly I was surprised any of my senses still worked. It was whiskey. Some kind of blended version, if I had to guess.

Great. Just perfect. Burly Hugh looked more and more like a drunk who had crawled into the diner to sleep off a bender.

I found an empty spray bottle by the sink and filled it with water. Positioning myself on the opposite side of the checkout counter (just in case I needed to make a run for it), I leaned over the top and proceeded to spritz the unconscious man. The mist must have been too fine, because other than the rise and fall of his chest, he still didn't move.

Crawling farther up onto the counter, I stretched my arms over the other side, hovering just inches from his face. I pumped the trigger hard three or four times, then screamed and dropped the bottle when his hand shot up and grabbed my wrist. The Neanderthal yanked me completely over the top and onto his naked self. He growled— honest to goodness, I wouldn't lie about such a thing. He growled. The noise started in his chest. I know, because I could feel it in mine, which was now crushed against him.

Why hadn't I just left and called the police? It would have been the easy thing to do—the smart thing. His arms were squeezed tight around me, and I became acutely aware of his Mr. Happy pressing against the skin of my thigh.

His eyelids cracked a peep, then he narrowed his gaze. "Who are you?"

"I..." I should be the one asking the damn questions, but the only ones coming to mind were completely inappropriate. Like, where did he work out? How good looking were his parents to create such a fine specimen of man? And did he have a girlfriend?

There was a moment, a very weak moment on my part, where I began to lower my face to his, our lips only centimeters apart.

*What the hell am I doing?* Where was my head? He could be a serial killer, a rapist, or someone *really* bad, like an Amway salesman. I turned my head away from his.

"Could you let me up, please?"

He squeezed me tighter. "Are you going to answer me?"

Finally, I gulped and squeaked out, "Sunny Haddock."

His left eyebrow rose. "Sunny Haddock?"

"Uh, that would be me. Yes." I'd been in town less than an hour and I was already famous. Well, my name was on the side of the building. "And you would be?"

"Babel Trimmel."

"Chav's baby brother?" I'd heard stories about him, but I'd imagined him to be terminally twelve. The age he'd been when Chav had left Missouri for the West Coast.

"Chavvie made a big mistake. She shouldn't have asked you out here."

Talk about judging someone before you get the know them. Barely through introductions and he already wanted me out. I've made a bad first impression before, but what the fuck? What didn't he like about me?

Although maybe it wasn't about like. Because, by the rise of his hoo-ha against my leg, I could swear he liked me a little.

An unfamiliar flutter twittered in my stomach. It'd been awhile since I'd been so physically attracted to anyone. Babel's nostrils flared with a slight huff. His brows narrowed. His eyes dark with purpose. I felt like Little Red Riding Hood, and Babel filled the role of the Big Bad Wolf intent on eating my goody basket. Oh, if only.

*Pull yourself together, Sunny.* But it was really hard, along with his arms, his chest, his abs, his...

Holding me tighter, his arms locked around me. He stroked my back with his firm hands. I trembled, fighting back a deep moan. "Please let me up, Babel," I said again.

He froze for a second then relaxed. He unlocked his arms from around me and smiled. "Call me Babe. Everybody does."

To say I scrambled off his body would be a bit of an overstatement. The trembling had left my arms and knees weak, but I managed, albeit slowly. "I don't know you well enough to call you Babe. Sorry." I couldn't keep my eyes off his semi-erect package.

"Could you put some clothes on? I'm feeling a little..."

He propped up on an elbow like a *Playgirl* centerfold and grinned. "Overdressed?"

*What an egomaniac!* "No. Sheesh." Okay, so maybe I felt a tad overdressed, even in my pink spaghetti-strap shirt dress with black short-shorts and sandals. It was

185

hot in Missouri. Sticky hot. And besides, I'd put in more hours than I care to count at the gym to counterbalance my donut habit, so I deserved to wear those shorts. My exercise routine wasn't all about the donuts. Over a year of no sex, since the dickhead had cheated, and while I'm no sex maniac, that's a long time for someone who had been getting it on the reg.

The "no sex" could also explain why I had such a visceral reaction to this guy. No doubt the man was a hunka-hunka. "Could you quit posing on the floor?" I wagged my finger toward his poker. "And for the love of daisies, put some clothes on before that thing puts out someone's eye."

He had the courtesy to look the tiniest bit embarrassed. "Nothing personal. It's a purely physical reaction."

"I'm sure you say that to all the girls."

"Sorry, I just meant, well, I'm a guy. You brush against the junk, it goes stiff."

"And here I thought I was special." This line of conversation bordered on hurting my feelings. I know I'm not a beauty queen, but neither am I Medusa. "You can shut up now."

Color rose to his cheeks—those nice fuzzy, chiseled, scruffy, manly cheeks, so perfectly bookending his Roman nose and gorgeous bow lips. And damn it to hell, his teeth were friggin' perfect! He pulled himself up by grabbing the counter, and holy schmoly, the man was tall. If I had to guess, he bordered on 6'5". I'm pretty sure I hated him for being so beautifully handsome.

"I only meant to say..."

I almost offered to buy him a shovel, but he managed to dig his own hole quite deep without any help from me. "I've got it already, jeesh. Not interested, physical reaction, yadda, yadda, yadda. No need to explain yourself further. Besides, I'm not looking for a boyfriend, so doesn't matter. And even if I were, it certainly wouldn't be my best friend's baby brother. We cool?" I didn't wait for him to answer. I waved him off. "Great. Excellent. Awesome even. Now, put on some damn clothes." Why-oh-why was I attracted to crazy?

"Perhaps you could find me a diaper."

Guess he didn't like the "baby" comment. Oh well. Sucks to be him.

He covered himself with his hands. Thank God. However, it didn't stop me from checking out the rest of his body. *Ay Chihuahua!* Damn, it kind of sucked to be me.

I knew from Chav that Babel had moved back to Kansas City where their parents lived after he'd taken a year off from university to look for their brother Judah. What was he still doing here? A horrible thought entered my head. "If you're here, does that mean..."

His face suddenly sobered. "I don't know. Mom and Dad haven't been able to get ahold of her for the last couple of days, so they sent me down to check in. I got here yesterday."

"She texted me a couple of days ago. I haven't been able to get ahold of her since then." I lifted a hand to comfort him, but his nakedness stopped me from breaching the distance. "Babel, we're going to find her." Even if I had to turn over every stump and stone in this backward-ass town.

"Call me Babe. Everyone does."

That was the second time he'd said that to me, but I couldn't call him Babe. No way, no how. Too intimate. Especially since I'd seen him in his birthday suit. "I don't think so."

He chuckled, low and sexy, and everything went right south of my navel. "Sunny,

I'm afraid I've, err...lost my clothes."

"You've got to be kidding me." How did a person go about losing all their damn clothes? "Fine. I'll stay on one side of the counter. You stay on the other. Kapeesh?"

"I understand," he said with a practiced tolerance. It made me wonder who he'd gotten so much practice with.

He hadn't turned around yet, and part of me felt really sad about it. I'm sure he had a killer butt to go with his killer bod. I was all about the teeth and ass. But there were no complaints about the whole frontal part of him either, so...

"Good. Should I call someone for you? Or do you want to call someone? A girlfriend? Anyone who can bring you some clothes?" Subtle. Not.

"The phone's not working here even if I could call someone."

I noticed he'd didn't say "no girlfriend." Much to my annoyance, I cared. And why was the phone turned off? "Don't you have a cell phone that works?"

He moved his hands, indicating his lack of attire. "No pockets."

In the immortal words of Homer Simpson, *Doh*! I snuck another quick glance at his dangly bits, even more annoyed with myself for not having better self-control. "Great. Fantastic." I waved my hand again and purposefully looked away. I had a cell phone out in my truck, and was just about to tell him I'd go get it when he stepped out from behind the counter, still full Monty. "Hey! Keep the mammoth covered."

"Flattering. But there's nothing prehistoric about it." He cocked his eyebrow and smirked.

*Bastard.*

"Look here, darling." He pointed to his "junk" as he'd called it and said, "This here is what you call a penis. It's connected to the bladder and the bladder is full. Turn your head if you want, sweetheart, but I'm heading to the john."

"Lovely. And I'm not your darling." I made a show of rolling my eyes and turning away. "I'm going to get my cell phone. I expect you to be standing behind the counter by the time I get back." Now, for the sake of posterity—well, at least for the sake of his posterior—I glanced back as he headed left to the bathroom. Of course, it was sort of hard to notice his ass when I saw the— "Blood..." I whispered.

A pain pierced my temple as my knees buckled beneath me. I dropped to the ground. My peripheral vision narrowed to black. The pounding of blood racing through my arteries swelled loudly in my ears. It was out of beat with my heart.

The thumping of blood stopped, my eyesight began to clear, and I was in Babel's arms.

"Sunny? You okay?" I heard his voice as a muffled echo.

No, I wanted to tell him. I wasn't okay. But my mouth didn't work. A vision came over me. I could sense it like death come knocking. Then I was no longer in Babel's arms. I was a ghost. A spectator.

*I was...in a shabby apartment with furniture dating back to the seventies? Had I traveled to the past? It wasn't unheard of for me, but it couldn't be relevant for something in my life now since I hadn't been born until 1974. Or could it? Great. The powers that be were giving me a psychic reading on my lost Crissy doll. Useless.*

*I heard a muffled cry, maybe a scream from beyond the front door. I passed through and down the stairs. The noise grew louder. Animalistic growls and snarls. Fear tightened in my stomach.*

*It's not real, I reminded myself several times as the feral sounds made me shiver.*

*I couldn't see any creature, but it certainly sounded like someone was getting voraciously attacked. And the room—it looked familiar. Two windows high up on the far wall spilled moonlight across the floor to...the counter? This was the restaurant. The noise continued, loud, animalistic, with grunting, groaning, and a masculine "ah!" Oh. Oh no.*

*If I'd really been there, I'd have run, but the vision took me closer to the scene of the crime. On the floor, behind the counter, a gorgeous woman with long dark hair, golden eyes, and even in the bad lighting, a body I'd give my right tit for, straddled the very naked and very sexy Babel Trimmel. I wanted to gouge out my eyes. Where was a hot poker salesman when you needed him?*

*The woman threw her head back and laughed. "You were fantastic, Babe. As always."*

*He smiled, his eyes rolling back a little. Coming up on his elbows, he leaned his left shoulder forward and looked behind. "You've got to do something about those fingernails."*

*"Just marking my territory."*

*Holy smack, the blood on the floor had happened during sexcapades? Yikes.*

*"I'm not your territory, Sheila."*

*The woman, Sheila apparently, picked up a bottle of Canadian Mist from the floor beside them, took a swig, then dumped some of the amber liquid down his large chest. No wonder the place reeked.*

*Babel shook his head and gave her thigh a light slap. "It's time to go, Sheila. I've got to get the place cleaned up."*

*"You sure you don't want to move here?" She licked his nipple. "I've sure missed you."*

*He sighed. The sigh sounded like it'd been one that he'd perfected over and over for this very argument. "It's not this town or you. I've got a real life out* there.*" He said "there" as though he was talking about an alien planet. "I'm going to find my sister, then get back to it."*

*"And what if you don't find her?" Sheila asked. "You never found Judah."*

*Babel's eyes narrowed. "Not an option," he said. Then*

191

added, "I'm finding her, and after, getting the heck out of this town. It's brought nothing but bad luck for my family."

"Sorry," she said, as if she wasn't sorry, an evil smile playing on her lips. Okay, so maybe more mischievous than evil, but it was my vision, I could use whatever adjectives I liked. "But you know that answer pisses me off."

Before he could blink, she whacked him super hard across the temple with the bottle of blended whiskey, and Babel was out like a light.

"Bastard," Sheila muttered. Which I understood, because it had been my sentiment exactly.

She dressed quickly, gathered up Babel's clothes, and walked into the kitchen area. It was small, but nice. I hadn't had a chance to see it yet, so it was like my very own psychic tour. She opened the walk-in freezer and chucked the jeans, boots, socks, and T-shirt inside. No underwear. Huh. I'd file that nugget away for later.

My vision stopped with her slamming the front door, and suddenly I was back, looking up from the floor at the towering and still very naked Babel. "Ow." My head, my back, my butt—everything hurt. "Did you drop me?"

"What the hell just happened?" He looked a little freaked out.

I got up on my elbows and rubbed the back of my skull. "Did you drop me on the ground?"

"You were having a seizure or something. I laid you on the floor." He was definitely freaked. "If I'd had a phone I'd have called for the doc, but..."

"I'm fine now. You can stop worrying." I moved my feet off the chair Babel had propped them up on.

"I'm sorry. I'm squeamish about blood."

Which wasn't a complete lie. Blood tended to bring on funky psychic mojo that left me drained and pained. Although, I'll admit, these visions had been much stronger than normal. Apparently, Chavvah wasn't the only Trimmel who put my psychic stuff on speed dial.

"I'm getting that about you." At least he sounded less upset.

I closed my eyes. "Why would you let someone do that to your back?"

"That's a story for another day, darlin'."

Yeah, I knew the story. Not so sure I wanted the blow-by-blow again. I felt his arms go under me, and I opened my eyes, staring into the deep abyss of his gorgeous, Midwest baby blues.

I let him carry me upstairs to the apartment. I'm not a small woman, but he held me like I weighed next to nothing, which made me think kindlier of him. With my arms around his shoulders, I could smell an unidentifiable musk and spice to his skin. He sat me down on a couch—the scent went from musky to musty—then he went into another room. I heard water running in the sink. More than a whisper of regret passed through me. I barely knew the man and I missed being in his arms. I looked around the living room.

This was the seventies place where my vision had started. The retro decor lacked any sophistication that could've made the space sensational. I knew this had been where Judah lived when he'd been in town. He'd rented this building before his disappearance, and Chav had used our stake to purchase it during her search for him. His vanishing had hit her hard.

Chav told me once that she hadn't agreed with her oldest brother's "lifestyle choice," but she respected him. I'd asked her what she meant, but she had shaken her head, unwilling to elaborate. I knew it wasn't as simple as him being gay or anything like that, because Chav, like myself, was socially liberal. Hell, she'd have started her own PFLAG (Parents, Families, and Friends of Lesbians and Gays) in Peculiar if that had been the case. No. There was something else she hadn't approved of.

I heard the water turn off in the kitchen. Babel returned and proceeded to wipe my face and neck with a cool cloth.

"There now, all better." For a second, he sounded like my father. Which totally squicked me, considering the hard-core fantasies I had about him. He put the washcloth in my hand and patted my shoulder. "I'm going to jump in the shower real quick. I'll be back in a few."

Part of me wanted to watch him walk away strictly for the view, but since that part seemed to have done gone and lost its damn mind, I waited until I heard water running before looking in his direction.

He'd left the bathroom door open. Perv.

I couldn't believe it, less than an hour in a new town and I'd witnessed a *Red Shoe Diary* moment, and the star was lathering up less than ten feet away. I would've been downright disgusted by the whole morning if I hadn't been so preoccupied with thoughts of slippery suds sliding along his perfectly formed pecs. (Now I understand how bad porn gets started. Bow chick-a bow-wow.)

*I will not go stare at the naked man.* I repeated this mantra in my head over and over as I ran down the stairs to the kitchen.

Grabbing his clothes from the freezer, I contemplated where they'd been and how they got there as I carried them back upstairs. They were cold and held the scent of sweat, but at least he'd have something to put on so he could go away. I placed them on the couch, and dear Lord, it was a really ugly couch. It would be the first piece of furniture to go when Chav and I started fixing the place up. And with that thought, I went downstairs to wait for him.

Fifteen minutes later, the light flickered on in the stairwell. Babel's arms and face glistened with dewy goodness as he walked down the steps. He rubbed a tea towel, barely big enough to dry a fish's butt, against his loose mane of wet hair. His blue T-shirt clung to his chest. Water soaking through the fabric made spots the color of midnight.

He must have felt me staring, because he dropped his arm to his side and looked at me. "Where'd you find my clothes?"

"The freezer." I wrapped my knuckle on the counter. "Guess you can go home now."

"Guess so." He shrugged as he stretched his body to tuck in his shirt. "But we should probably talk."

"I'm in no mood." *For talk.* Damn, he was super-fine.

"Well, you kind of need to get in the mood." He

195

shook his hair out, droplets spraying out around him. It began to feel like a bad (or really good, depending on who you asked) shampoo commercial. "There's been a mistake. My sister should've never invited you out here, Sunny."

"You've said that already, but unfortunately for you, my name's on the property, same as hers, all legal and binding. I'm staying. Period. End of discussion. Besides, I'm not going anywhere until I find Chav."

Babel chewed his lower lip and narrowed his eyes at me. "I don't think you understand the situation."

"Oh, I think I do. You don't like me. Fine. I get that."

"It's a might more complicated than that." He scratched at his five o'clock shadow.

I resisted the temptation to offer him a hand. "Why do you care, anyway? Don't you have a *real* life you want to get back to? You seem awfully concerned for a guy who isn't even sticking around."

"And what makes you think that?" Babel asked.

"Uh..." Fair question. I couldn't exactly tell him that I'd heard him tell his cuh-razy lover in a vision. "Well, you didn't exactly stick around after the search was called off for Judah."

A pained expression crossed his face. I instantly regretted being such an ass. It was a low blow, and petty even.

"I stayed for as long as I could stand it." He shook his head. "I'm not meant for this place, Sunny. And neither are you."

Another twinge. "It doesn't matter." We would find

Chavvah, then he would be gone. "Have you heard anything? Are the police searching for her?"

"No and yes. I haven't heard from Chavvie, but Sheriff Taylor isn't giving up." He flicked his thumbnail against his ring fingernail. "Not yet, anyways."

"She'll show up, Babel. I just know it." But I didn't know it. In my heart, I believed she was alive, and not because of any vision. "She's my best friend. I'd feel it if she was gone. Now, go on back to wherever you're staying..." Oh, crap. Maybe he'd been staying here. "You do have another place to stay don't you?"

Babel nodded once. "I've been staying at Chavvie's cabin down by the lake."

"Good," I whispered. I'd want to check out her place later for clues to what happened. "It's been a long drive for me, and I need a nap so I can figure out what I have to do next to find her."

He shook his head as if he was having an argument with himself. "I'll be back in a couple of hours with some cleaning supplies and get the floor behind the counter scrubbed."

I didn't want to talk anymore. I wanted to get my bags out of the truck. I'd hassle with unpacking the U-Haul later, but the bags were a must. I needed something personal, something of mine in this place. I held out my hand. "That's a nice offer. I can manage. Thanks."

Babel took my hand, and gave me a tight-lipped smile. "You don't handle blood very well. After I clean it up, maybe we can compare notes about Chavvie."

I nodded, afraid that if I spoke the dams would open

197

and I wouldn't be able to stop the tears. Then I heard a voice like a whisper in my ear.

*Save her.*

Babel let go of my hand. "I'll be back." The way he said it sounded more like a threat than a promise. As he walked out the front door, he added, "You've got an audience."

**Get this book from your favorite eTailer!**

# PARANORMAL MYSTERIES & ROMANCES

## BY RENEE GEORGE

**Nora Black Midlife Psychic Mysteries**

Sense & Scent Ability (Book 1)

For Whom the Smell Tolls (Book 2)

War of the Noses (Book 3)

Aroma With A View (Book 4)

Spice and Prejudice (Book 5)

Age of Inno-Scents (Book 6)

Aroma Holiday (Book 7)

Vapes of Wrath (Book 8)

The Scented Cipher (Book 9)

**Grimoires of a Middle-aged Witch**

Earth Spells Are Easy (Book 1)

Spell On Fire (Book 2)

When the Spells Blows (Book 3)

Spell Over Troubled Water (Book 4)

Ghost in the Spell (Book 5)

**Destiny of a Middle-aged Witch**

Burning Djinn of Fire (Book 1)

Djinn Bottle Blues (Book 2)

Stand By Your Djinn (Book 3)


**Peculiar Mysteries & Romances**

You've Got Tail (Book 1)

My Furry Valentine (Book 2)

Thank You For Not Shifting (Book 3)

My Hairy Halloween (Book 4)

In the Midnight Howl (Book 5)

Furred Lines (Book 6)

My Wolfy Wedding (Book 7)

Who Let The Wolves Out? (Book 8)

My Thanksgiving Faux Paw (Book 9)


**Witchin' Impossible Paranormal Mysteries**

Witchin' Impossible (Book 1)

Rogue Coven (Book 2)

Familiar Protocol (Booke 3)

Mr & Mrs. Shift (Book 4)

FurOut (Book 5)


**Barkside of the Moon Paranormal Mysteries**

Pit Perfect Murder (Book 1)

Murder & The Money Pit (Book 2)

The Pit List Murders (Book 3)

Pit & Miss Murder (Book 4)

The Prune Pit Murder (Book 5)

Two Pits and A Little Murder (Book 6)

Pits and Pieces of Murder (Book 7)

Pittie Party Murder (Book 8)

## Hex Drive

Hex Me, Baby, One More Time (Book 1)

Oops, I Hexed It Again (Book 2)

I Want Your Hex (Book 3)

Hex Me With Your Best Shot (Book 4)

Hex Me All Night Long (Book 5)

# About the Author

I am a USA Today Bestselling author who writes paranormal mysteries and romances because I love all things whodunit, Otherworldly, and weird. Also, I wish my pittie, the adorable Kona Princess Warrior and my two cats Ash and Simon could talk. Or at least be more like Scooby-Doo and help me unmask villains at the haunted house up the street.

When I'm not writing about mystery-solving were-cougars or the adventures of a hapless psychic living among shapeshifters, I am preyed upon by stray kittens who end up living in my house because I can't say no to those sweet, furry faces. (Someone stop telling them where I live!)

I live in Mid-Missouri with my family and I spend my non-writing time doing really cool stuff...like watching TV and cleaning up dog poop

### Follow Renee!
Bookbub
Renee's Rebel Readers FB Group
Newsletter